Gemini

A Beyond Fairytales story

By
Catherine Peace

Copyright © 2016 by Catherine Peace
ISBN: 978-1-61333-998-5
Front cover art by Syneca Featherstone

Published by Decadent Publishing Company, LLC
Look for us online at:
www.decadentpublishing.com

Dedication

To Landra and Marisol, for keeping me sane, and to Raven for helping me wrangle Uri.

Prologue

After his second failed expedition in two weeks, Uriah Jacobs settled down for a pint at the nearest watering hole on Fahiri, one of the few planets in the Argos system that catered to humans, though a few of its countries still had a ban on receiving human goods. He chuckled to himself then took a drink of the warm ale he'd been served. Swill, but it'd do its duty.

Behind him, a small stage had been set up with a stool and a microphone. "Any idea what that's about?" he asked the barkeep.

The large fahir, basically a human-sized cat, shook its head. "Old man, storyteller." It shrugged, and Uri noted the way it tried to mimic humans, the latest fad to reach the system, he presumed. "Been making the rounds, I guess."

A storyteller. Might be interesting. He swiveled around and crossed his ankle over the opposite knee.

After a few minutes, a small man, really more imp than man, hobbled onto the stage. An untamed white beard extended to his knees, and deep wrinkles limned the uncovered portion of his face, as though he'd lived a hundred lifetimes in one. Then Uri noticed the man's legs, how they bent in the back like a bird's rather than a man's, and he shuddered. What sort of man was this?

Using a steel pipe to help him up on the stool, the old man settled and turned to the microphone. "Lads and ladies, my name is Nicodemus," he said, in a strong voice belying his stature. "I be a traveling bard, a collector of stories from across both time and space." He leaned forward and a large blue spider

1

emerged from his beard. Instinctively, Uri reached for his gun, but once the spider settled on Nicodemus's shoulder, he relaxed. "And, tonight, I have a story for ye. For a few coins, of course."

A chuckle rippled through the crowd. Two patrons stood and placed a couple of coins on the stage at the base of the stool.

"Ah, thank ye. Your kindness is astounding." The imp cleared his throat. "Allow me to begin. It is a tale of tragedy and heartbreak, twins separated from each other, from the only family and safety they'd ever known, indentured to a cruel master called Nix."

Uri froze.

"Brother and sister, each put to a different task, each uncertain of their place in this strange new world, both dreaming of escape." This time, the old man looked straight at Uriah. "A tale some of you know all too well."

Placing his pint glass back on the bar, he rose to leave. No need to hear the imp's tale tonight. No need to involve himself. *It's only a story.*

"Komandan," the old man said, stopping Uri in his tracks, "you may want to return to your seat."

"I've no need of this," he replied.

"No. But *she* does. Return to your seat."

Heat flooded Uri's body. She? She who? The sister? *This is a story*, he reminded himself. *The old man needs more coin.* Without a retort, he sat back down. A crooked smile on the storyteller's face, he continued his tale. "Once upon a time...."

Chapter One

"Balls!" Uri screamed. The dials on his console spun out of control while the ship careened toward Goliv, a place he knew all too well. As he breached the atmosphere, sweat beaded on his forehead and his heart climbed into his throat. *Not here. Anywhere but here.*

He brought the ship to rest near an encampment. He swiped a hand through his coarse hair and tried to force down the memories of his own imprisonment, working the forge for hours, sometimes days, at a time to thread wire. These nyx would just as soon hold him hostage and demand a ransom from the Embassy. Out in the sticks like this, they'd leave the Embassy no choice. Every human life mattered to them. Even his.

Or maybe they'd re-enslave him, Komandan or no. Just the passing thought iced his blood.

It figured *Sea Snake* would fail him in the nyxen-dominated sector. If Ambassador Stormbringer hadn't sent him.... He'd give her a piece of his mind later...and then beg forgiveness, as always. After all, she'd protected him from a fate far worse than anything the fish heads might concoct. His freedom belonged to her.

He ejected and hopped down onto crunchy rock. All around him extended a vast expanse of gray nothing, except for the rock outcroppings that gave the landscape its only visual appeal. A perfect canvas, Ambassador Stormbringer had said. To him, the one advantage Goliv had over every other planet in this sector was its atmosphere. Before the nyx took it over, the Embassy had planned to terra-form it and give humans a better place to live than abandoned space stations or hastily constructed safe zones, but, like with so much, they failed to reach a consensus. Stepping into camp, he spotted one of the nyx in its enormous bodysuit. Damned oversized blowfish. Had to be the result of fish coming out of the oceans millions of years ago to walk on land. "Hail," he said, hoping his translator chip still worked.

The alien turned to face him, pulse rifle trained on him. It tensed. "Name."

Even through the speaker, he caught the tremor in its voice and bit back a laugh. Must've been a new guard, one who somehow didn't know about the human who'd escaped nyx slavery. Some of the universe's most creative storytellers claimed that humans were indestructible, meaning Mr. Fishy probably thought the pulse rifle useless and depended on intimidation.

"My name is Komandan Uriah Jacobs. I've had some issues with my ship. Hoping to get some assistance." The last words tasted like acid; he had to refrain from spitting on the dusty ground.

The nyx visibly relaxed.

"Where is your *Vodja*?"

"Follow me."

***

For a species known as the galaxy's cheapskates, the *Vodja*'s living space boasted more luxury than he'd ever seen in the Embassy, which surprised him, considering most of the fish considered "warm-blood" luxuries to be useless. Uri had gone to the nyx home world once—more than enough times for him. Lophus, the armpit of the universe as far as he was concerned, had little to no industry; the entire species depended on claiming other planets and exploiting mineral sources or metals or whatever else they found. And because of the limitations from their suits, they had to use slaves to do it.

He followed Scared-y Nyx back into the meeting room, trying to forget the last time he'd walked this route. Through a child's eyes, everything had seemed enormous, terrifying. Through an adult's, it all further enraged him. If he had any hope of getting off this damned rock, he had no choice but to play nice.

As he entered the meeting room, the guards flanking each side of the nyx leader hesitated, but the blue-scaled blowfish didn't flinch. "Uri," it said before introductions were made. "What a surprise."

Balls. It'd been a long time since his turn in the fish's labor camp, but this one had been especially brutal. And somehow, Evirax had become *Vodja. Galactic justice at its finest.* "A pleasure to see you, too."

It *hmph*ed. "Freedom has not been good to you."

It's only a disguise. Making himself look older and grizzled helped him earn respect from the other Komandan, as though he embodied the stories they'd heard about humans.

"What brings you to my colony?"

Colony, labor camp, all the same. "Ship malfunction."

If these things registered surprise, he had no doubt he'd shocked the hell out of Evirax. "Have your own ship?"

"Komandan."

From the change in the air, he'd impressed his former master.

"The Embassy's pirates don't pass through this sector much. What have you been doing in nyx space?"

He'd asked himself the same question before his ship decided to retire without notifying him. "The Embassy received reports of some interesting artifacts. They sent me to look into it." He shrugged. "Didn't pan out."

The fish leaned forward and rested a mechanical arm on its mechanical knee—imitating a human, as though the action put them on equal footing. Even under their control, Uri had always had the advantage. "How about I help you, if you help me?"

"Help you how?"

"Give me a cut of your...profits? Half, maybe?"

Extortion? "When did you become so greedy, Evirax?"

"The better I do, the better you do."

Uri crossed his arms over his chest and pretended his heart wasn't about to pound through his rib cage. Half his profits? No deal. But he couldn't get the *Snake* fixed without Evirax's help. Damned if he did, probably re-enslaved if he didn't. "You have a deal."

***

Shadi splashed cool liquid on her face, though the goop did nothing to alleviate the heat still clawing at her neck and back. Tiny droplets of perspiration barely caressed her skin before evaporating in the forge's heat. The other workers had already left for the evening, abandoning her yet again to another long night of soldering and threading wires. She stretched her sore fingers and cracked her knuckles. Outside the door, one of the nyx stood guard, ready to intervene if it thought she wasn't working her fingers to the bone. Though they were tough on all the workers, they were especially hard on her. Over the years, other aliens had come and gone through the forge's blazing heat, but she hadn't seen another like her since her brother's transfer. Still, she held on to Ezra's promise he'd come for her and rescue her and Shilah from captivity. She just had to hold on a little while longer.

She returned to the workstation, wishing for a glass of actual water. None of the others understood her yearning for water, as though the idea of hydrogen and oxygen creating something so glorious never crossed their minds. Their lizard DNA prevented them from enduring the forge's heat for long, meaning she often worked alone. Most of the time, she didn't mind it, but, tonight, the loneliness crept in. The calendar she kept for herself, measured in Earth units—an archaic method of time-mapping since Earth no longer existed, but one she'd learned on the ship and kept to—marked the twelfth year since she and her brother were separated and the fifteenth since they'd been sold. Still, she kept faith.

Sometime later, a shadow fell over her workstation. One of the nyx, in its titanium suit, stood in the doorway, a mess of strange sounds coming through the speaker in the center. Shadi narrowed her eyes. In her captivity, she'd learned to read the nyx through these odd noises, which she'd used to piece together a language. The hisses and gurgles were all she knew, and since these creatures were incapable of facial expressions, they were all she had. After a moment, it turned back around as though to leave then swiveled back toward her. She supposed they needed her. And when they needed her, something was usually broken.

***

She hadn't expected a ship, at least not one so...pieced together. An old Class-II scorpion-tail cruiser that might've held two people and a small captain's quarters, it appeared to have been converted somewhere along the way, upgraded in ways that didn't matter in the end. Certainly lacked any sort of cosmetic upgrades. The patchwork hull sported plenty of dings and pockmarks from space debris, and the windscreen needed replacing as soon as possible, though she could probably reseal it and make it last long enough for the pilot to reach safety.

Curiosity got the better of her where the pilot was concerned. If ships required her expertise, they belonged to traders the nyx leader wanted to impress. Regardless of her ignorance concerning their language, she'd learned to associate the ships with the traders. This was not a trader ship.

Or a slaver ship.

Before getting into the nuts and bolts of the scorpion, she looked around for the pilot but found more nyx and a couple of her fellow slaves preparing to bunk down for the evening. As she worked, the guard grabbed a luminary and flicked it on. The tiny machine whirred to life and perched on her shoulder, providing more light than anything else she'd seen. "Thank you," she said.

The nyx gurgled a response that she hoped was, "You're welcome." No sense in being rude.

After a few minutes of searching, she located the issue—a cooling coil that had gone bad and caused a blowout through the rest of the engine. Not a difficult fix, but it'd be time consuming. She sighed and rolled her shoulders. Time to get to work.

Chapter Two

Never in his life had Uri thought he'd be on the receiving end of nyx hospitality. Though his stomach rumbled, he refused the food they offered—perfect for a dextro-based alien, but toxic to a human. Once the conversation turned back toward business, Evirax forgot about the slight. "I may have one or two good leads from the Embassy," he said. "If I can uncover something, I should receive a decent payment for it."

As he expected, the alien made an approving noise, bulbous eyes struggling to stare at him. What had he feared as a child? If he punctured the faceplate of the helmet, the gloop inside would spill out and his former master would suffocate before it even hit the table. A fabulous option if he had need of it.

"You'll do well, Uri. You don't have a choice. My best mechanic is repairing your ship. Your ship will be better than new, faster, stronger."

"You must have a hell of a mechanic."

"I do. She's the only one I've had that's lasted the forge." It leaned forward. "You remember what it's like there, don't you?"

He did, and if she could tolerate the forge's heat.... "She's human?"

"Your species is more resilient than anyone truly knows. I tested your mettle and found you lacking."

"I escaped."

The fish head continued as though Uri hadn't spoken. "I've had her for nearly six cycles, and she's the strongest worker I've got. Never complains." A static-like sound came through the speaker. "Doesn't say a damn word. You'd never shut up."

"I'm opinionated," he growled.

"Ah, speaking of...."

Turning in his chair, he spotted another nyx, but behind it stood a girl, probably no more than twenty-one, if he was being generous. Her lank brown hair reached to her waist, and her clothes, more soot and holes than actual garments, hung on her malnourished frame. She reminded him of the day he'd had enough, killed the nyx guarding him, and taken off in one of their ships. Still, her dark-green eyes sparkled with knowledge. In her filthy hand, she held a part from *Sea Snake*.

At first, she didn't notice him. She laid the part on the table in front of Evirax and waited while working the inside of her jaw. The *Vodja* looked from her to the part and back again. "It's bad," she said.

"The hell is this?" Evirax studied the part and then threw it back down a few seconds later.

"It's a cooling coil," Uri supplied. With a gasp, the girl met his gaze. "So that's why everything went to shi—. Rubbish. Why it went to rubbish." He smiled at her, but she continued gaping at him like *he* was the alien.

"Find her one of these." Sitting back, Evirax's tiny fish body swam in anxious circles in its glass prison. After the girl and the guard left, it settled down.

"You know, you'll be in deep shit if the Embassy hears of this."

"Maybe," it said in a tone exhibiting calm. "But they won't, will they?"

"No. They won't." *I'll do you one better*.

***

He has to be working with Ezra. He's keeping his promise.

Shadi kept her pace steady, but her heart beat a frenetic rhythm that had every part of her body shaking. Soon, they'd be reunited and then they could search for Shilah. *I'll find you, I swear I will*, she thought, the same words Ezra had said to her the night before she'd ended up in the slave camp. She could still smell the whisky on his breath. He'd drunk so much in the weeks leading up to the sale....

The guard led her to the storage warehouse. The luminary perched on her shoulder took flight and shone its light at full brightness. A glorified scrapheap, parts from all kinds of ships ended up in the warehouse one way or another. As she sifted through the piles, she hummed an old song Ezra used to sing to get her to sleep. A while later, she found a coil that would work in the scorpion-tail. Time to get the ship operational.

As she stepped around the scorpion-tail's innards littering the ground, she tied her hair into a loose knot and got to work, still humming Ezra's lullaby. She perched on the lip of the ship, the luminary hovering around her head. The guard acted as a makeshift tool belt and handed her what she needed. Saved her time from having to hop down. Besides, she liked this one, as much as someone could like something she couldn't communicate with.

By the time she finished, taking extra care to thoroughly clean the parts before she reinstalled them, darkness hovered on the horizon. She switched off the luminary and smiled at the guard, which swam in a quick circle as if to say, "You're welcome."

Maybe I'll miss you, she thought.

***

3

Full dark never touched Goliv, but the nyx kept to a rigid schedule. With any luck, he'd only have to kill one or two in his effort to rescue the girl while the rest powered down their suits for a few hours of slumber.

After his meeting, he'd taken a self-guided tour around the encampment. Certainly not a memory lane he wanted to traverse, but he had to re-familiarize himself with the locations and guard patrols if he meant to do this quickly and quietly. *Sea Snake* waited for him, no doubt purring better than the day he bought her, and he wanted the hell off this damn rock. They'd travel to Dalara, where he'd procure new IDs, get her cleaned up, and shuck this ratty disguise.

He slid around a construct and scanned the area for fish heads. So far, so good. The air was quiet, like it held its breath in anticipation of the great escape. It'd *be* a great escape if he could convince her to leave.

***

Shadi rolled around on her small cot, and her hands kept brushing against the hard stones. By the ache in her knuckles, she'd have more than a few scratches to show for her poor night of sleep. The anticipation killed her.

Ezra. Soon. Soon she'd look into his kind blue eyes again. She'd hear his whisky-roughened voice tell her how proud he was of her for lasting so long in the forge, that he loved her. In her excitement, she kept envisioning the reunion, the rescue, having the two most important people in her heart back in her life. They'd be a family again, thanks to the man.

4

But then another theory scurried across her mind, leaving tiny footprints of doubt. What if he was just another slaver? Then he'd take her to another camp. All this time working on nyx ships had familiarized her with the way most vessels operated, and she'd spent enough time poking around his. If necessary, she'd take it and find her brother.

She slipped on her boots, which had holes in the tops and almost no bottoms left, and after ensuring the other slaves still slept, she crept out of the tent. Disappointment coursed through her, thanks to her stray thoughts. The man's deep voice and kind smile gave her shivers in unexpected places, but if he intended to take her to another camp....

No. He worked with Ezra. End of discussion.

First, she had to find him.

In the quiet, she heard a purring noise. *The ship. He must already be there.* Stepping carefully, she tried not to make a sound, but she couldn't hide the prints left in the dusty ground. *I'm coming, Brother. Hold on.*

She'd nearly reached the line. Up ahead, maybe a few yards away, the ship gleamed bronze in the muted daylight. Heart hammering against her ribs, she almost took off in a dead sprint, but a mechanical hand grabbed her shoulder and held her in place. The hissing coming from the guard's speaker didn't sound good for her, and she had no excuse to offer.

Pain shot through her shoulder and down her arm as the creature increased the pressure of its grip; if it didn't let up, it'd shatter her bones. She let out an agonized scream that burned her throat raw, sounding more like an animal from one of Ezra's vids than anything she recalled as human.

"Let her go."

The nyx hissed again, but it released her. Gripping her shoulder with her left hand, she skittered out of the way behind a rock outcropping. The human stood with his pistol drawn on the alien. Sweat glistened on his dark skin, and he watched every movement the alien made to placate him. But she knew their tactics well. It'd appease him and then shoot. She'd seen it play out so many times in pantomime between species. As he began to lower the pistol, she panicked. "It'll still shoot," she blurted.

Only the barest hint of a nod showed he understood. In a swift movement, he raised his pistol and shot, the sound almost deafening in the stillness. The glass faceplate shattered and thick, clear liquid spilled from the opening. The nyx tumbled to the ground, deceptively small body flopping around on the dirt. All this time, she'd never known how fragile her masters were.

The man turned his attention to her. "Are you hurt?"

"My shoulder...."

He nodded. "I can help you, if you'll let me. But we need to move quickly. Other nyx will be coming."

She took his proffered hand, and he helped her from her position behind the outcropping. *Soon.*

***

Before either of them spoke again, he made sure the ship broke Goliv's orbit. From above, the planet didn't look so hideous, and Shadi couldn't tell where the forge was. The relief that cascaded through her left her exhausted.

"We're heading to Dalara," he said. "A doctor may need to look at your shoulder."

"Okay."

"And we can get food there."

She hoped for something softer than what the nyx had offered. "And then we'll meet Ezra?"

When he narrowed his eyes at her, her heart sank. Fear strengthened her system, emboldened her in a way it never had with the nyx. "He sent you."

The man blinked once, slowly. She vaguely remembered Liam doing the same when she'd confused him with her made-up stories and saw a resemblance between them she hadn't before. "No," he said. "No one sent me."

"But you're *human*."

"He didn't send me."

"Liar," she whispered. Sometimes Liam would play games with her, tell her things that weren't real. Ezra would reprimand him for it, and Judah would snicker in the background. "You're lying. You have to be."

"I'm not," he said gently.

Then I'm not staying. She retreated to the sleeping room. He wouldn't get to see the tears in her eyes.

Chapter Three

On the ship, Shadi kept to herself, curled into a ball on the softest cot she'd ever laid on, unable to sleep. The engine's hum lulled her into a doze, but every other sound she heard pulled her back into full alertness. She expected one of the nyx to kick her awake. When no one came, she was both grateful and concerned.

Eventually, she headed to the cockpit where the Komandan sat in quiet repose. Sitting in the vacant copilot's chair, she studied him. Scars marred his forearms, and she saw the markings of hard work on his hands, same as hers. In his face, she read weariness and a small trace of fear around the tightness of his eyes. She reached to touch a thick strand of coarse gray hair, but before her fingertips made contact, he jerked awake, as though from a dream. Or a nightmare.

She brought her knees against her chest and tried to hide behind them, as she'd hidden behind Shilah when they first stepped onto Goliv. Like then, she didn't know what to expect; she only knew wires and spaceships, not humans.

"Have you been able to rest?" he asked, wiping sleep from his eyes. She averted her gaze to the console, where the displays remained steady, and shook her head. "I see. Are you hungry?"

"Yes." She ran her tongue along her chipped and broken teeth.

For a moment, the man's eyes didn't leave her face, and she shrank back from the scrutiny. The nyx only cared about her ability to work. What was he looking for in her?

8

"What's your name, girl?"

"Shadi. From an old language Ezra liked." A smile pulled at her lips. The day Ezra named her and Shilah was one of the fondest memories she had.

"Now, girl, we can't keep callin' ya 'brother' and 'sister.' You need good names." Ezra pulled her onto his knee and fussed with the too-big shirt one of the crew had given her. "Strong names," he said. She smelled the whisky on his breath, a sweet scent. "Shadi. You like that?"

She nodded. She liked having a name all her own.

"Tell me about him." He reclined in the swivel seat, crossed one leg over the opposite knee. Though his clothes were unremarkable, they were cleaner than she expected. No tears or tatters. No evidence of repairs. However, hers were to the point of being held together by whatever thread she could find. Sometimes spare wiring.

"He was...." How to describe him? Broad shoulders and stubble, close-cropped white hair and crow's feet stamped beside his ice-blue eyes. Friend. Family. "He sold my brother and me to the nyx." And he'd been the one to leave her and Shilah with audio players of vocabulary lessons so they'd know how to speak, what things were. Some things, she didn't have words for. Like the "food" the nyx forced her to eat or the gloop that had imitated water. Or the feeling she got when she looked at the man in the other chair. "He didn't want to, though," she added quickly. "He loved us. He said he'd come back for us."

The Komandan took in everything she said with eyes like Ezra's—full of hope and despair.

A few breaths of silence passed, and Shadi began to squirm, desperate for a way to fill in the gaps of conversation. His voice filled her head with music in an accent she didn't recognize. Ezra's voice had been roughened by years of cigarettes, Judah's often flat and monotone, but his? Lyrical. "May I ask your name?"

When his posture relaxed further, she congratulated herself for remembering the audio file concerning polite behavior. Regardless of how angry she was at the moment, Ezra had stressed the importance of good manners, and she wouldn't let him down.

"It's Uri. Uri Jacobs." Turning back toward the console, he scrubbed a hand over his face. "Why don't you try lying down again?"

"The cot is too soft," she replied without thinking.

He nodded. "You're welcome to try the floor if you like. I'll work on a more suitable arrangement."

Uri watched her go before exhaling and sinking further into his chair. He remembered Shadi's Ezra perfectly. Ex-military, tough as hell, full of vim and whisky. The day they met was a day he'd never forget.

He had no issue with leaving Ambassador Stormbringer an anonymous tip. None at all. If those assholes got thrown under the jail, he wouldn't shed a tear. And the worst of it? This man she seemed to idolize would have sold her again, and again, and again if he had to relive those moments.

For now, all Uri had to do was get her to Dalara.

First, he had to reach out to his contact. From muscle memory, he typed in Vani's comm code. After a few moments, his friend's large black eyes and rust-colored face filled the screen. "Let me guess. Ready to ditch your awful disguise?"

"Yes. For the love of all that's good. Also.... I have a guest."

"Who'd you piss off this time?" his friend asked.

"Probably a few dozen nyx."

He expected the gurita's silence. Whereas humans were often regaled as the most dangerous species in known space, nyx *were* the most dangerous species. Not because of strength or superior intellect, but because of their numbers and sheer determination. "What. Did. You. Do?"

"Nothing major, really. Killed one, took off with their human slave." He cleared his throat. "She's the guest, by the way."

"Why do you hate me?"

"Think of it as me keeping you on your toes. We'll need IDs, and she needs to see a physician. You can arrange that, can't you?"

"Of course," Vani replied, though the incredulous look on his face remained. "One new ID for stolen property coming up."

He cut the comm, leaving Uri seething at his calling Shadi property. He adjusted the throttle and opened *Sea Snake* wide to add the speed they'd require to outrun Evirax. Then a new thought struck him; he dialed his friend again. Before the gurita could say anything, he said, "The *Snake* will need a few upgrades as well."

Chapter Four

Admittedly, Uri hadn't been paying attention to the console. When the fuel gauge slipped between a quarter of a tank and E, he almost went into a full panic. They still had almost a week's travel before they reached Dalara. *Balls.* Any delay gave Evirax an opportunity to catch up, take them by surprise. Take Shadi. *No.* Never would he allow another woman to suffer under nyx rule.

According to his map, the next closest fuel station lay within reach of their nearly exhausted supply. He breathed a sigh of relief. Fuel stations provided more security than landing on a planet for supplies, especially in this quadrant. Dalara wasn't the safest planet in the galaxy, but, compared to its neighbors, it might as well have been the Embassy.

He glanced back toward the cabin where Shadi had holed up. The girl hadn't been out for a little while, and he hoped she was okay. No need to disturb her, though. She needed what rest she could get.

His first few days of freedom hadn't gone much better. He vaguely remembered stealing one of the nyx's ships in the dead of night, though he failed to remember what colony he'd been working on, and somehow landing on Dalara—crash landing, more like—near Vani's store. The gurita had suggested he take on the role of Komandan, and once he'd explained what a Komandan did, Uri agreed. Working as a treasure seeker for the Embassy sounded far safer than trying to fend for himself.

What kind of life could they procure for the girl? Obviously, she'd make a good mechanic. The *Sea Snake* operated better now than the day he bought her. But she'd been working on ships since her childhood. Would she want a change?

There's time for all that. Just get her safe, first.

***

Pacing the small room did nothing to calm her nerves. She'd never been cooped up for so long. Torture. Worse than the nyx. If they confined her, they typically let her out within hours. By her guess, days had passed.

Still, being on this tiny ship beat working in the forge.

However, her skin tingled like tiny bugs were crawling on it. Anticipation. Nerves. Something.

A desire to find her brother. The need to see him again took over everything in her, leading her to walk in tight circles in the sleeping room. What would freedom be without him?

She wished for Ezra's guidance. More than that, she wished for a chance to find Shilah herself. Being beholden to someone else, whether human or nyx, did nothing to help her. Surely on her own she had a better chance.

A soft knock on the door pulled her out of her thoughts. "Shadi? We're making a pit stop for fuel and some supplies. I'll find you something to eat, but you need to stay aboard the ship. No one can know you're here. Okay?"

"Okay," she replied, but she was already planning her escape.

***

She waited until the engines died, leaving the ship far too quiet for her taste, and listened for Uri's footsteps to disappear. She had one shot. One chance.

For all she knew, this might be her last chance. The Komandan had never given her a reason for stealing her from the nyx.

Unfortunately, she found nothing to use as a weapon, but the added risk didn't deter her. Once she knew she was alone, she poked her head out of the bedroom to confirm, and then she stepped into a world of light and sound.

Everywhere she looked, blinding messages flashed on the sides of buildings and people filled every crevice and available area. Ships whirred in and out, almost deafening in the domed space. She'd been to one of these stations once, only a few days before they were sold. Ezra had made certain she clutched his hand while they passed through the crowds. He'd even bought her and her brother candy.

No one gave her a second glance while she slipped through the throngs of people. Too many were jabbering in their languages, and, for a moment, she missed Uri's calm, soft voice. Shaking it off, she headed toward a clear area to catch her breath, take note of the fueling station, maybe find a place to hide while she watched the ships come in and out, decide which might be easiest to steal. Without any idea what her brother was going through, she *had* to get to him. Had to know he was safe, okay. Alive.

The idea that Shilah hadn't survived the nyx lived in the back of her mind, and on occasion, it surfaced, attacking her in the night or during those moments when she thought her brain to be calm. Though she never entertained the idea for long, she knew it to be a distinct possibility. The forge had never been kind to her; neither had the aliens who demanded so much from her.

She pushed forward toward an area with a smaller concentration of people. From there, she planned to climb to higher ground and get a better idea of what she faced.

A tall alien brushed against her and grabbed her by the wrist. Heart in her throat, she gazed from his coppery fingers and black claws up his well-muscled arm to a cruel grin full of sharp teeth. The curved black horns on either side of his head caught the fluero-light from the floating lanterns decorating the station. He muttered something, at which his companion, a tiny creature barely reaching her knee, laughed. She pulled against his grip but might as well have been struggling against any of the buildings surrounding her. This had never happened with Ezra. For the first time, she understood his obsession with age and mortality. "Let go," she said. This time, both aliens laughed. Shadi looked between them. The one holding her had a definite weight advantage, but the smaller one wouldn't be an issue after one well-placed kick. If she weren't so damn weak....

What had she done?

A click sounded next to the tall alien's shoulder, and he went rigid. The smaller alien stepped back, buggy eyes wider than she thought possible.

"Let her go."

Uri. Relief and anger warred within her. She hadn't even had a chance to find a ship. Hadn't done anything.

The tall alien released her arm, and she nearly fell to the ground. Before her rescuer-slash-captor could assist her, she caught her balance and stood up straight. For a moment, she and Uri stared at one another; she failed to translate the emotion in his eyes. He didn't look at her like the nyx did when she disobeyed them. In fact, she couldn't quite place the look he currently gave her. It stirred something within her, another something she lacked a name for. "We need to get back to the ship," he said.

Like she'd done nothing wrong. Like she hadn't

tried to leave him behind.

Unable to stop herself, she asked, "No punishments?"

"That isn't your life anymore," he said, his voice soft. "Now come. I found something for you to eat."

Chapter Five

A knock pulled Shadi from the most restful sleep she'd had in a long time. When they returned to the *Snake*, she'd eaten her fill of the foods Uri brought her and then she'd hidden in the sleeping room. No mention of her escape or of punishments or anything. Weird. So weird. She wondered if she'd ever get used to him. To any of this.

The blankets she'd commandeered from the cot pooled at her waist, and she rubbed the sleep from her eyes like Uri had done before. The small gestures they shared warmed her. No aliens had ever wiped the sleep away, and she always considered herself an outsider because of the human gestures that earned her strange looks. Still, she needed to guard herself. Ezra had imparted his wisdom before the bay door closed and cut her off from him. "Watch out for yourself and for each other," he'd said. "And don't trust anyone who isn't your twin."

The door slid open, revealing an exhausted-looking Komandan. Bags hung under his unfocused eyes. "We'll land on Dalara in a few minutes," he said. "They'll do a cargo check. Stay calm, and don't say a word."

She nodded, and when he motioned for her to follow, she did. "If anyone asks, you're a mechanic who helped me with my ship in exchange for a ride here." He reached into a small locker and handed her a hat. "Put your hair up. No mechanic would keep her hair down. Might get caught in gears."

"I know that." Her hair concealed, she shivered with both excitement and trepidation. She'd never thought about seeing another planet, though, as

17

children, she and Shilah had tried to imagine the planets their fellow slaves had come from and made up stories about their home worlds. After he was sold, she continued the game for a while, but it was too boring without his wild imagination. And, now, she only had to sit through a cargo check to set foot on another planet. Amazing.

He returned to the captain's chair and pressed the button flashing bright green on the console. A robotic voice filtered through the speakers, nothing like the hisses and globs of the nyx. "Prepare for cargo check. Please have cargo manifest and invoices ready."

"No cargo, no paperwork." To her, he said, "This won't take long."

"Okay."

She vaguely remembered the cargo checks on the other ship. They were the only time Judah and Ezra forced the twins into the hold with the other slaves; she never got to go on-world afterward.

As the pair of bots boarded the cruiser, she sat in the co-pilot seat and waited for them to perform their scans, the anticipation of leaving the ship almost overwhelming her. The first bot scanned Uri while the other headed toward the very back.

"Komandan Uriah Jacobs, please present manifest."

"I've no cargo to claim," he answered in his smooth, proper voice full of music.

The bot made a dissatisfied beep and then turned to her. "Stand."

Glancing at Uri, who offered a reassuring smile, she got to her feet, stomach churning. It repeated the process, scanning her from head to toe, except it let out a shrieking beep. *"Unauthorized cargo."*

"Shit!" Uri grabbed her by the arm. "Run!"

With his hand firmly around her wrist, she

followed.

The beeping and bellowing sounded right on their heels. Uri dragged Shadi through crowded streets and alleyways in a zig-zag path to Vani's, he hoped. The girl panted and stumbled once or twice, but she kept pace. Amazing how much strength a person could muster when her life was on the line.

When the noises disappeared from his ears, he stopped to catch his breath. Sweat dotted Shadi's face and her dark-green eyes were wide with fear. Along the way, she'd lost the hat. Without another thought, he brushed strands of hair from her face. "It's not much farther," he said. "Can you make it?"

"Yes."

"Good."

***

Vani's home was packed between a fetish store and meat market and seemed to change every time Uri came back. The gurita's legitimate business of ship repair services made use of the thousands of vessels making port at the settlement at any given time, but his true skill lay in forgery.

He sat behind a desk, making notes and yelling at his other workers. Shadi's eyes narrowed, and she stilled for a moment, listening. "Do you have a translator chip?" Uri asked.

She replied with a sullen shake of her head, and he added the invaluable device to his mental list.

Moments later, Vani glanced up from his desk; his bug-like eyes widened at the girl. "I see why you brought her. She looks like...well, like you did that first time."

He nodded. "Glad you see my side. She'll need a translator chip. Can you procure one?"

"Sure thing. By the way, what happened to your ship?"

"Probably impounded by now. Had a minor run-in with security." His face heated. "She's still listed as cargo."

The alien made a sort of squawking sound, which was apparently the human equivalent of a face palm. "Well, great. I can try to get it out."

Casting a sidelong glance at his companion, he said, "We don't have that kind of time. Any way to get a new ship?"

"You're lucky I like you." A few swipes of his tentacles, and he glanced up. "I can get you one. You'll owe me big time for it."

"Just put it on my tab."

"Your tab's as long as my—"

"That's quite enough."

Vani shrugged. "Not like she can understand me, anyway."

Uri shook his head. "Shadi, are you hungry?"

Without looking away from the gurita, she nodded. He took her by the wrist again and led her to a console in the back of the shop, painfully aware of the clock ticking down in his mind, every valuable second whittling away. "Show me your teeth."

For a second, she hesitated. Then she opened a mouth full of cracked and broken teeth. "The doctor will repair them." He hoped he sounded reassuring; the fear still hadn't left her eyes. "Once we get your new ID, we won't have any other difficulties. You'll have to think about where you want to go." Pressing the food-options button and selecting levo-amino acid, he chose two bowls of soup and water.

"Go?" she asked.

Once the selection was confirmed, he palmed her gaunt cheek, surprised by her smooth skin. "The universe will be yours. I can take you back to your family or make other arrangements. Wherever you want to go, I'll take you."

Chapter Six

And leave me there. Or maybe he'd tire of her and leave her on Dalara with his strange alien friend. She stepped out of his touch, regardless of how much she enjoyed it. All of this was too overwhelming, too much at once. "Why did you take me?" she asked.

A steely mask settled over his face, and the hard glint in his eyes unsettled her. "I'll tell you over dinner." He paused. "Which will be here any moment."

Sure enough, a ding came from the front. Admittedly, she couldn't wait to try actual human food. At this point, the gloop had to be the only thing keeping her going; she'd given up on the hard biscuits years ago.

Uri disappeared and reappeared just as quickly with two containers and bottles of clear liquid. Not gloop. "Chicken noodle," he said with a sheepish grin. "Does the body and soul good."

Whatever that meant.

They found a secluded spot with a small table and sat down. "You owe me a story," she said.

"I do, indeed." He opened the lid on one of the containers. "Here."

The soup smelled like salt. She looked at the bits and pieces floating around in the...stuff.

"Try it," he urged.

She watched him use a small scoop-like utensil to dip into the container and tried to mimic him. For her troubles, she got a bit of liquid and a green thing. Then she took a small sip and her eyes widened at the taste. So much better than rocks.

"What do you think?"

22

"It's good." Not a strong enough word, but the right one escaped her. Or maybe she didn't know it yet.

He smiled, and she marveled at how bright it was, how perfect his teeth and...well...him. Suddenly, the gray hair seemed out of place.

Mouth full of soup, she nodded. The green things were delicious.

"When I was fourteen, raiders attacked my colony, searching for a mineral deposit rumored to be hidden in our mountains. Once they discovered we had no such mineral deposit, they chose to take what we had an abundance of—humans, which might have been just as profitable, if not more so. A long and bloody standoff ensued, and enough people died to orphan most of the children. These raiders turned out to be human, too."

A lump formed in her throat. Suddenly without an appetite, she pushed the bowl to the center of the table and waited for him to either confirm or dispel her fears.

The wait seemed endless while her companion mulled over his words. Indecision dulled his eyes. "Tell me it wasn't him," she whispered, unable to bear the silence.

He snapped out of his memory. "I can't. One of our own suggested selling humans, and Ezra Welles agreed. They turned to the slave trade that day. I hoped they'd find the egregiousness of selling their own kind intolerable, but," he said with a weary sigh, "I see they haven't."

"Ezra wanted to stop," she blurted. "I know he did." She wiped tears from her cheeks. "He cried for me and Shilah. He loved us. Swore he'd come back."

"Even so, he proved he loved money more."

Enough. Shadi pushed back from the table, unapologetic when a bottle spilled. "You didn't know him." Then she stood and headed for the door. Maybe it'd be best if he left her behind after all.

His conscience pushed him to pursue her. Danger lurked in every part of Dalara, and anyone who found her wandering the streets might do worse than tell her the truth about a man she adored.

In a flash, he caught up with her. He placed a hand on her shoulder, and she stopped but didn't turn around. "I shouldn't have—"

She whirled around, fire lighting her eyes. Another heartbeat had her raising her fist. In one fluid movement, he pinned her wrists to her sides and pushed her against the wall. And he decided that, yes, even broken, she was beautiful.

"I hate you," she whispered.

"I don't blame you." Whatever he'd gotten himself into, he needed to get himself out—quick— but this girl had already pulled him into her orbit. "Listen to me, Shadi, carefully." She struggled; he answered by pressing his body flush to hers, and she stilled. Mouth next to her ear, he said, "People here will try to hurt you. Hate me all you like, but stay with me until you're safe."

A tiny sob shook her petite frame. No doubt, he'd shattered her with what he'd said about her beloved Ezra. Honestly, he had no way to reconcile the man he knew with the father figure she'd described.

"Hey, you two, doctor's here."

"Thanks, Vani." Uri stepped back enough to see her face. "Just a little while longer," he said to her. The fire in her eyes abated some, but the hard set to her jaw remained. "Let's get you to the doctor. We need to start moving again soon."

She nodded. He let her walk away, sure to stay close behind. On Dalara, one could never be too careful.

Chapter Seven

She didn't know if she hated Uri, but she loathed knowing he was near. While the doctor, an alien she'd never seen, checked her over, she silently fumed. Worst of all, she had to stay with him until....

Until when? The doctor prodded her ribs, jabbed her twice with needles, and took some of her blood while Uri watched and translated. Once she got her translator chip, she wouldn't need him anymore. She'd be able to find her brother on her own.

"He wants you to stick out your tongue. Open your mouth wide."

She did, if only to make the process move faster.

Dr. Alien's tiny eyes didn't look like they'd see much. His entire face was scrunched like he'd tasted something sour, like those candies Judah enjoyed, the ones Shilah always helped him eat. Afterward, her brother always got a stomachache, but he didn't care. Uri had called the doctor a veruta, but she didn't know what that meant, if anything. At the moment, she had trouble allocating worth to anything the Komandan said.

"It won't take long to repair your teeth. You have a severe vitamin deficiency, though." As the doctor lifted a large syringe filled with a shimmery gold liquid, Uri continued. "The syringe contains enough to help your body start repairing itself. With a suitable diet, you'll gain weight and eventually start feeling better. We'll have to start slowly, though, since your body isn't used to the vitamins and minerals it needs."

Sounded like gibberish. Like she'd be stuck with him until some undetermined time when her body decided to cooperate. Would she need him to stay with her in case she had some strange reaction? The idea of stealing a ship and striking out on her own seemed further and further away.

And after what'd happened in the hallway, less appealing.

Damn her body for betraying her mind.

"How long 'til we can leave?"

Her companion—for the time—worked the inside of his jaw. "It may be days yet."

"Do you think the nyx will find us before then?"

"No," he answered too quickly.

"You don't sound sure." Before he could defend himself, she said, "You've been here before. Maybe several times. You knew exactly where we were going, how to avoid the main streets, where the food machine was, and I can tell you and Vani have known each other for a long time."

"Shadi, I—"

"They'll know we came here," she said. "They'll search for us here."

After a few minutes of tense silence, Uri dipped his head once. "You're right, on all accounts. They will come looking here." He stood, and at his full height, while she sat on the exam table with her hands between her knees, he was an intimidating force, not just a pirate. "But what they won't account for this time is my willingness to fight." With one last glance to the doctor, he left.

The veruta injected her with the gold liquid and her veins burned. Then he grabbed a tall, thin metal stand and affixed a clear bag to it. Suddenly, she missed Uri; without him to translate, everything the doctor did held a menacing note. He slid a tiny needle affixed with a tube into her hand and said something. A few moments later, he injected her with another syringe, and she fell asleep.

***

Storming out had to be a bad idea, and he shouldn't have left her alone with someone she couldn't understand, but her intuitiveness unsettled him. How much had Ezra Welles taught her before abandoning her on Goliv?

Or maybe she had a natural gift. Maybe she'd always been able to read her companions in such a way, analyzing tics and verbal cues to create a different sort of language, but one effective enough to help her survive. After all, she'd known the nyx would shoot first.

His fist connected with the wall, and the ache in his bones dulled the ache of frustration gathering force at his temples. Damn Welles for letting this girl rot away, and damn him for thinking this a simple rescue.

When the door opened again over an hour later, and Shadi emerged with brighter, though troubled, eyes, he met her gaze head on. "Are you okay?"

"I know where I want to go," she said.

By the hard set of her mouth and the determination blazing from her, he didn't think he'd like the answer. "Where?"

"To find Shilah. I want to find my brother."

Find him, meaning she didn't know where he was. "Any idea of where to start?"

She deflated a tiny bit. "No."

"He may not be a slave anymore, Shadi. Maybe he escaped and is making a new life elsewhere."

"Not without me. He'd come back for me. I know it."

Who was he to convince her otherwise? Just because his own brother handed him over to Ezra Welles personally.... "Are you sure about this? We'll

27

have to work together to find him."

Her determination didn't waver. "I will do anything it takes to get my brother back. You made me a promise, pirate."

"I did, and I will uphold it, I assure you. For now, we need to get cleaned up. How is your mouth?"

She smiled wide and without mirth, showing off her new teeth. "It hurts."

"You'll be sore for some time. Simply means we can order more soup."

A grin played with her lips. There was hope, after all.

Chapter Eight

After a long, hot shower, Uri removed the last vestiges of his useless disguise. The ink comprising his false tattoos had disappeared in the swirl of water down the drain, and the prosthetics that created the crow's feet around his eyes and lines around his lips sat on the sink until he decided if he wanted to reuse or discard them. Time for the dreadlocks.

He glared at his reflection. Whose idea had these been? Oh, yes. Vani's. He'd have to thank the gurita later. And by thank, he meant strangle.

Another half hour and he looked himself again. Younger, though with the same weariness around the eyes and natural crow's feet, which were less pronounced but still noticeable. He stepped away from the sink and tossed the chunks of hair in the trash, already trying to think up a cleverer disguise. He had to be able to fool the nyx if it came down to it. Knowing them, it would.

Once he slipped into his regular clothes, he joined Vani at the front of the store. "Ah, there he is," the gurita said. "Looking better already."

"Your crummy disguise didn't work."

Vani made a strangled sound. "You just didn't commit." After flipping down the lid to his laptop, he studied Uri for a few uncomfortable moments. "No one besides me knows what you actually look like. That's your best disguise. The one you might actually stick to."

The thought hadn't crossed his mind before. All he cared about was staying below nyx radar, rather than ending up right on it. "With a new ship...."

"A change of name *and* a beautiful new wife. Mr.

Oliver Hall, representative of the humans of the Athens Grove system," he said, handing Uri a photo ID card, "has officially wed the lovely Leida Welles."

"*What*?" Leida Welles? Where did Vani come up with any of this?

As if hearing the questions bouncing around Uri's mind, the crafty alien began to laugh, which was a series of short coughing sounds. "You ought to see your face right now."

"How did you manage this?"

"You don't need to know. But these identities will serve to get your asses off this rock. Go on, start thanking me and praising my genius."

"Welles."

Rolling his globular eyes, he sat forward. "You humans. So single-minded. Stop focusing on minor details."

"The last thing I need is Ezra Welles breathing down my neck. I'm trying to get Shadi *away* from slavers, not deliver her to them."

"He won't, and you won't. I've been tailing Ezra's ship. You guys are operating in totally different quadrants."

"For now." Suddenly, the seat became unbearable. As he stood and popped his back, he turned away from Vani to face the front of the store. Just beyond the door, two aliens were engaged in a heated argument. The tone of their words permeated the door, but what they were saying didn't.

Vani perked up. "I guess Ora and Noot are into it again."

At least it wasn't anyone connected to the nyx. "They regulars?"

"Live in the shit hole across the street. This entire neighborhood is a shit hole."

Uri's pulse hadn't yet slowed. Danger lurked in every shadow, and he couldn't stop the fear of discovery from icing his blood. "Any news on a ship?"

"Demanding." A smirk on his face, Vani opened his laptop again and pressed a few keys. Then he turned the screen around. "Here's your new baby."

A sleek black cruiser filled the screen. Sitting back down, Uri—now Mr. Oliver Hall—looked at the specs of the ship. Shaped like a stingray from Earth, it promised speed and evasiveness, both of which he'd need to outrun the nyx.

"What Pratt Dynamics' website doesn't tell you," Vani said, smirk still in place, "is that these E-class cruisers come with some significant upgrades if you toss a certain name around." He tapped a couple of keys and the screen changed. "Check this out."

An email from PD's CEO.

Mr. Vani, we are more than happy to meet Mrs. Welles-Hall's desire to upgrade the chosen E-class cruiser with the chosen specifications. Attached, you will find more information to pass on to your client. We will endeavor to make the cruiser available as soon as possible. Per Mrs. Welles-Hall's request, we will not disclose these upgrades to the Embassy.

Unable to believe the amount of power the Welles' name held in the universe, Uri tapped the screen to open the attachments. "What have I been missing about Ezra all these years?"

"It's not so much Ezra as his son. Judah is a formidable asshole. While you've been slumming in the Sol system, which *I* avoid like the damn plague, he's been building an empire. Now he has a nice front to fund his flesh peddling."

"Which is?"

"He owns a mining enterprise. Has a near monopoly on taralsite, which companies like PD need to build higher-capacity drive cores to power awesome ships like this one." He turned the monitor around. "You'll have to name her."

"*Gemini*," he said, remembering some old Earth astrology. Surely a ship named for the sign of twins would help him reunite them. "How soon can she fly?"

"As soon as you need her to. You'll pick up the keys at the lot."

***

Hot water. It was enough to have actual water, but the warmth loosened the knots in her muscles. She couldn't remember the last time she'd had a shower. Maybe she never had.

This definitely beat the pond where she'd bathed once a week. Instead of icy...not exactly water...chilling her to the point where she welcomed the forge's heat, this contraption kept her standing under a waterfall of perfection. Her fingers had long past reached the point of prunes.

When she finally pulled away, she was caught by the reflection in the mirror. A different girl stared back at her, one whose eyes were wide with fear, as they always were, but Shadi spotted a flicker of hope. She smiled, still taken aback by her repaired teeth, and part of her hoped for Uri's approval. *Stupid*, she chided herself. Seeing another human had addled her brain.

Before she entered the bathroom, Vani had gifted her with a new set of clothes, finer than anything she'd seen—a white button-down shirt with lace collar and wide sleeves and a pair of olive-green loose-fitting trousers. She tightened the belt she'd been provided around her waist, slipped on a pair of soft leather boots, ran her fingers through her gloriously-clean hair one more time, and stepped outside. A rush of air chilled her. Up front, it'd be warmer.

32

The man standing with her new friend sucked in a breath when he saw her. Only by his eyes did she recognize Uri. Heat crept into her cheeks. She'd thought him handsome before, but with his cropped black hair, perfect dark skin, and the clothes accenting his lean frame, she couldn't stop looking at him. And he couldn't stop looking at her. Glancing up and down her body, he made a slightly strangled-sounding noise and then cleared his throat.

"You guys are adorable," Vani said. "Which is why you're married now. Mrs. Leida Welles-Hall, meet your husband, Mr. Oliver Hall."

Chapter Nine

Married?

Shadi stepped back and planted herself against the wall, the only support she found on such short notice. Married. To Uri. She glanced between them, unsure of where to focus or who to query. Exasperated, she stared at the floor. "Why?"

"It's easier—and safer—for a married couple to travel alone." Vani shrugged, as though it was the simplest answer in the universe.

"Not the marriage," she said, though she'd questioned that, too. "The name."

Though her memories were whispers more than anything, she vaguely remembered Ezra talking about his daughter, Leida, how he never saw her because of his sister. Back then, she couldn't fathom keeping anyone or anything from Shilah, but she understood a lot of things now. "If Ezra hears her name, he'll come running for her. Choose a different one."

"He can't."

She glared at Uri, who leaned against a support column, arms crossed over his muscular chest. "Why not?"

"To make the ID, he needed someone who had a valid identification number."

Meaning Ezra's daughter was alive somewhere, and if he didn't know where.... "He'll come after us. If they scan me at port again, somehow he'll find out."

The gurita shrugged. "It's too late, kiddo. You and your new hubby have a ship to pick up."

In futility, her eyes met Uri's, and she almost willed him to say something, *anything,* to vocalize

34

how horrible an idea this was. He remained silent.

"Fine. We need to get moving."

She wriggled her fingers. The *wedding ring* Vani had procured almost cut off circulation to her finger. No matter how she twisted or turned it, it still bit into her skin, regardless of its almost-perfect fit. "Must I always wear this?"

Uri squeezed the hand he held in an iron grip, the one not encumbered with a stupid ring. While they walked, she glanced at their entwined hands, disgusted by his proximity. She hadn't yet decided if she had it in her to forgive him for destroying her memories of Ezra, or if she even should. "In public," he said lowly. "In private, you may do with it what you will."

Fair enough. "This still doesn't fix the problem with my ID."

"I know. One issue after another," he grumbled.

"Which means what? Ezra will come after us."

Stiffly, Uri nodded. He said nothing further.

***

The moment they were off-world, he'd explain everything. He'd tell Shadi about the plan to lure Welles out, that Vani intentionally chose Leida's name for her ID. The fear of Welles recapturing her plagued him more than the threat of the nyx and the knowledge of what would happen to her—to them both—if they were caught.... His stomach churned with the thought.

No matter what, he'd keep her safe. Somehow, he'd reunite her with her brother. And if he rid the galaxy of one of its chief slavers in the process, all the better.

Ahead of them, the ship lot gleamed like a

beacon of hope. They hadn't been followed, and few had spared a glance at them. As a center of trade, be it legal or otherwise, Dalara boasted all manner of travelers. Even dressed in the finery Vani had procured, they didn't stand out, but none of his mental reassurances soothed him. Every shadow, every wandering eye, every hushed conversation signaled danger. He refused to be caught unaware.

Attempting to keep their pace light, Uri scanned the ship lot in search of any sort of movement. Nyx did not play fair.

So far, so good. No movement in the shadows. No need to be quite so alert. Regardless, he kept his hand above the butt of his pistol.

He had to admit, they looked nothing like the pair who had escaped the *Sea Snake*, Shadi especially. From the corner of his eye, he looked her over, impressed by the change in her. She carried herself like a lady, chin held high, a little sway in her steps. She smiled at a few passersby, and his heart stuttered in his chest with the hope they'd be able to pull this off.

"Stay calm," he whispered to her. "We only have to pick up the ship. They'll likely speak to you, but if you need, I can take over."

Shadi dipped her head once but didn't say a word.

On the lot, he glanced around at the different ships, surprised by the selection. Toward the edge of the property, he spotted the ship Vani had procured for them. He pointed it out to her, and she stopped for a moment. "That's our ship?"

"Better than the *Snake*, eh?"

"Much."

"Ah, you must be Mr. And Mrs. Hall." A salesman, another gurita, welcomed them. He took Shadi's hand in his tentacle and attempted a shake. "I am Autjan. I worked with Mr. Vani on procuring the ship for you."

"And the upgrades?" Uri asked.

"Already installed and tested." Autjan gestured toward the ship. "Shall we?"

While the gurita talked about specs and the upgrades, and Shadi asked a few questions, Uri kept an eye out. By that point, the nyx had plenty of time to catch up, and no doubt, they'd been alerted by the port authority. The change in her ID would put distance between them, but it'd possibly bring the Welles' group closer. He prayed the plan he and Vani had hatched would work.

"Mr. Hall?"

He snapped to attention and glanced between the alien and his companion. "Yes?"

Shadi chuckled. "You'll have to excuse Oliver. Sometimes his mind wanders to the strangest places." Rising on her tiptoes, she planted a soft kiss on his cheek. "He asked if you approved the upgrades to the ship, darling."

"Oh, yes, yes, of course." He cleared his throat. "When will we be able to take her?"

"After you sign the paperwork."

***

"Do you think we have a chance?" Shadi asked.

At this point, Uri didn't know, but this ship amazed him. *She* amazed him. "I believe, once we figure out where your brother is, we'll have a fantastic chance." He hoped it'd soothe her; she'd been on edge since they left the lot.

"I hope so." Twisting the ring on her finger, she stared into the floor.

He rose from the captain's chair and knelt in front of her, taking her hand in both of his. "I promise you, we will find Shilah," he said, and he prayed it was a promise he could keep.

Chapter Ten

Lying on the floor of the main bedroom, Shadi stared at the ceiling and mulled over Uri's promise. So far, he'd not given her a reason to distrust him, but Ezra's words came back to her stronger and clearer than ever: "Trust no one but your twin."

Finally, she yanked the wedding ring from her finger and looked it over. Such a simple object, a gold circle with so much meaning in the right circumstances. However, the man helming this amazing cruiser was still a stranger; she had no one to depend on but herself.

Worst of all, she didn't know where to start. According to Uri, the nyx had dozens of colonies in this sector, and her brother could be at any one of them. Or dead. She hadn't voiced the thought, but it played in the back of her mind on repeat. *Shilah's dead. He's dead. You'll never see him again.*

"Stop!" She slammed her fists against the floor, used the ache to settle her mind. She'd know, right? If something had happened to Shilah, she'd know.

Until she had more information, she needed to stay with Uri. Her new ID made it nearly impossible for her to be on her own, and she wondered if that had been the reason for Vani's choice. To keep her with Uri.

Rather than lie on the floor and debate until her head exploded, she went back to the cabin and plopped down in the copilot's seat.

"I thought you were trying to sleep?"

"I did try. And I failed. Miserably." She huffed. "I'm...concerned."

Uri shifted in his chair and looked at her with

appraising eyes. The scrutiny forced her to make herself as small as possible. "About what?"

"Shilah."

For a moment, the Komandan simply breathed. While she berated herself for saying anything, he stared at the floor like it'd done something interesting. "Why your concern?"

"Why *not* my concern? I'm not stupid," she said, clutching the chair arms to maintain her control. "I know you chose this name for a reason. How will it help us find Shilah?"

The man relaxed against his seat, and she somehow resisted the urge to claw his eyes out. "It won't."

Shadi's restraint nearly snapped. "Then what is the point?" she bit out. She eyeballed Uri's gun, but he didn't seem to notice.

"The point is that, by taking you off Goliv, I made a pact to care for you, which I intend to keep. Right now, apart from the nyx, our biggest threat is the Welles' group. If they take either of us into custody again, we may end up somewhere far worse than the crusty rock you grew up on."

"So you wanted to bring them closer by giving me Leida Welles' ID? Ezra has been looking for her for years." *This makes no sense!*

"With this ship, and with the element of surprise, we can take the Welles' group down. We're within reasonable distance of the Embassy, Shadi. We can put an end to them once and for all." He leaned forward and placed a warm hand on her knee. "No more siblings separated for gain. The universe would be able to breathe again, the nyx crippled."

"And what of the nyx slaves?"

"I can't tell you. All I can do is ask you to trust me. Will you?"

She nodded. "For now. But, I assure you, I will

take this ship if I have to."

Not an idle threat, either. Once she retreated to the cabin, Uri took a deep breath and wondered for the thousandth time what he'd gotten himself into. He cared for the girl, but at what cost? Since *Sea Snake* was out of commission for good, he needed this ship, with its splendid armaments and its promise of speed. If he intended to keep them both safe, he had to be able to outgun or outrun any threat. A shame the biggest threat seemed to be occupying the captain's quarters at the moment.

Still, he couldn't blame her for wanting to find her brother, her only family as far as he knew. The fact that she and her brother had "grown up" on a slaver's ship meant they'd been sold young, and with youth came the opportunity to teach. Shadi's mechanical inclination made far more sense. Ezra had trained her so whoever bought her would continue to find her useful, and wouldn't use her for the wrong things. The idea made his skin crawl. Over his years of freedom, he'd witnessed too much horror to let anything happen to his new charge that was worse than what she'd already endured.

After setting the autopilot, Uri toyed with the wedding ring on his finger, twisting it and tugging at it just to put it back in its right place. He had made a promise to her, a vow, and thanks to Vani, he had a symbol of it to spur him forward. Without a second thought, he connected to the info-deck installed on the ship's main console and started searching. Nearly an hour later, he found his first useful bit of info.

The colony permits nyx purchased were for specific resources. Goliv produced wiring and cords, in addition to having a damn good mechanic. The mines of Ayslade produced the energy source necessary for the fish heads' bodysuits. As he scrolled through the information—all public as mandated by the Galactic Council—he realized he didn't have the necessary information regarding Shilah's skills. And he doubted Shadi wanted another heart-to-heart.

She'd need a gun, he decided, and he'd teach her to shoot. In this situation, she had to be completely prepared for anything, and who knew what the nyx had planned? As far as he was concerned, they'd gotten off too easy. The escape had gone too well, apart from the port incident. He shuddered. If he knew Evirax, the old fish head had someone on their tail.

Chapter Eleven

The ship's scream woke Shadi.

And it sounded like a horrible scream, a shriek of pain. She rushed to the cockpit, where Uri scrambled to fix the problem. "What's going on?" she asked.

"We were attacked," he replied without looking at her. "You may want to sit down."

A sudden jolt forced her into the copilot's chair. "Do you know who?" *Is it Judah?*

"Not entirely certain, but my fairest guess is the nyx."

Her heart sputtered. It was a matter of time before they caught up, but she refused to go back, not to Goliv. Not to any of the colonies. "What can I do?"

"Buckle up. We'll need to make an emergency landing."

"So whoever is chasing us can find us. Smart."

Finally, Uri glanced up, deep-brown eyes full of ire. "Where we can make our last defense. Do you know how to shoot?"

"No." *Of course not. Why would the nyx want a slave who might eventually kill them? Or escape?*

"I figured as much." Another jolt rocked the ship. "We'll have to land on Chorth. Maybe hide out somewhere."

"Why? Why not just hand me over to them?"

He looked at her as though she'd ripped his heart out. "What makes you suggest that?"

Because I'm a slave. Because I don't know how to be anything else. "Because I'm far more trouble than I'm worth and you're risking your life for a complete stranger." The ship quaked, but, remarkably, the electronics remained stable. "Vani

43

knew this might happen, didn't he?"

"His entire life revolves around preparation. In case you weren't aware, gurita are often worriers. It's how they've survived for so long."

Gemini lurched toward the nearest planet, Chorth, she assumed. She buckled up, brought her knees against her chest, and waited for the inevitable.

The controls weren't responding nearly as fast as he needed. He couldn't lose this ship, too. If he had any hope of keeping his promise to Shadi, he had to do everything in his power to keep *Gemini* operational, safe.

Once they broke into the thick cloud cover of Chorth's atmosphere, he switched on the cloaking mechanism. Thanks to refractors positioned all around the hull, the ship blended in with its surroundings, much like a chameleon, allowing him to search for a safe landing zone, away from any kind of port authority.

He glanced at Shadi, still curled up in the copilot's seat, and steeled his resolve. At least he'd shaken their tail, but for how long he didn't know. The nyx were persistent, and the bounty hunters they hired came with reputations best not repeated in mixed company. Before becoming a Komandan, he'd spent years outrunning and outgunning the nyx. The fish heads were not fans of losing their property.

He brought *Gemini* to rest near a section of what appeared to be abandoned warehouses. From what he remembered, Chorth had once been a bustling port area, but a few bad decisions by their council had rendered the planet almost entirely obsolete. Since then, the reputation it'd gained kept away all but the most desperate traders.

Grabbing Shadi's hand, he pulled her from the ship and into the row of abandoned warehouses.

44

Some were rotting and falling apart, others had mold or rats, but one near the very edge of the district had remained mostly intact. They ducked into it and climbed onto the rafters, which shifted and groaned beneath their weight.

For a long while, Uri listened to his companion's erratic breathing. He tried to take her hand again, but she pulled away from him, the glare in her eyes enough to chill him to the marrow. Maybe she blamed him for this. He wasn't here to win awards; he intended to help her find her brother, get them to a safe place, and go on with his life. If she needed to hate him to make the process easier, so be it.

Nearly an hour passed in a harsh silence. The wind rattled loose boards, caused others to creak. Something in his gut told him that whoever chased them was merely waiting for an opportunity to strike. Part of him hoped for Evirax. Nothing would please him more than ending the life of the creature who'd tormented him for so long then turned the same torment on another scared child.

"How much longer?" Shadi whispered.

"I don't know. I don't want to take any risks."

"You've been taking them this entire time. What's the difference now?"

He swallowed. "The difference is that a risk now would endanger you, and I refuse to do anything to cause you harm."

This time, she covered his hand with hers and squeezed but said nothing further.

With a sigh and a great deal of regret, he pulled away from her. "If something happens, I want you to go to the ship. No questions. Get off this planet and find your brother."

"Without you?" she asked, eyes wide.

"Without me." He kissed the back of her hand and climbed back across the rafters. They couldn't

45

stay here forever, in fear of whatever chased them. Time to become the predator rather than the prey.

He peeked through the slight opening between the warehouse's massive doors. The vantage point gave him a great view of where he'd parked the ship but not much else. At least, not without opening the door and risking being seen.

Of course, when a pair of large catlike eyes filled his field of vision, the risk became moot.

In the hopes he'd stun their pursuer, Uri stepped back, kicked the doors open, and readied his weapon. Unfortunately, the fahir wasn't stunned; the catlike creature also had catlike reflexes. It'd landed near the ship, and Uri prayed he wouldn't come into contact with it. If he failed to kill Evirax's bounty hunter, Shadi needed to get off-world. Whatever happened, she had to escape.

"Where's the girl," the bounty hunter asked.

"What girl?" Maybe, if he played it off, he'd frustrate the fahir enough for it to make a mistake.

It snorted. "Evirax told me you were dumb." In a flash, it raised its gun and fired. Uri barely had enough time to dodge the shot, which blasted a hole in the door behind him. "I won't ask again."

"I don't have her, Catgut."

It bristled at the insult. "You're a shit liar. Besides," it said, stepping forward, "I've been watching you since Dalara."

What? He'd been so careful....

"You've done good work with the girl, I admit. Maybe I'll have a bit of fun with her before I take her back to Goliv. Evirax just wants her alive. Didn't specify in what condition he got her."

"You won't get near enough."

"Tough words from a coward." The fahir shot again, and Uri realized it was missing on purpose.

"Am I part of your bargain with Evirax, too?"

46

With a snort, the creature replied, "For some reason, he wants you alive. Is willing to pay extra for it. But don't let me give you hope. I've always wanted to kill one of your kind. Whether it's you or her doesn't matter."

Son of a bitch. Evirax wanted to put him back in chains badly enough to pay for it. "We're a lot harder to kill than you think."

"Which means the kill will be so much more satisfying."

He'd never met an alien with no fear of humans. Even the nyx tended to keep their distance and relied on subjugation for control. This thing? No fear, which made it more dangerous and far more prone to making mistakes.

Attention still on his opponent, Uri shifted away from the door. He needed to draw the fahir as far from the warehouse as possible. Out of the corner of his eye, he spotted Shadi, half-hidden by shadows, watching him. *Please let her take the hint.* "Well," he said, "what good is a kill without a hunt?" Then he took off.

Chapter Twelve

What is he doing? Horrified, Shadi watched Uri run into the cluster of warehouses, the cat-creature hot on his heels. Then she looked at the space where the ship still sat concealed. He'd told her to take it, hadn't he? Told her to find her brother. She'd been waiting for exactly this opportunity, so why did she hesitate?

Instead of going to the ship, she followed the route he'd taken until she heard the sounds of a scuffle. Hidden behind a stack of crates, she barely kept her composure as the creature knocked Uri unconscious with a harsh, sickening blow to the head. It hoisted him over its shoulder like he weighed absolutely nothing and headed toward a small cruiser parked at the end of the row. One prize taken, which meant it'd be after her next.

Once she thought she was out of earshot, she sprinted to the ship and collapsed into the captain's chair. Pushing aside her fear, she studied the ship's controls and found them markedly similar to the nyx's. A bit of luck or Vani's careful planning, she didn't know, but this meant she could get off-world.

She started the engines and engaged the thrusters to get airborne. *Gemini* wobbled before it found its balance, a trademark of larger ships, and then it climbed upward. Shadi had been on ships before, but they'd lacked the sheer power of this one, and, for some reason, it felt even more powerful from the captain's chair. After she cleared the lower atmosphere and crested the upper, she eased the thrusters back and transferred the additional power to maintaining the ship's cloaking function. While

48

she couldn't wait to learn the ins and outs of the controls, she focused on the goal finally within her reach. Except....

She cursed, fingernails digging into the soft leather of the armrests, then opened up the comm channels and scanned them until she found Vani's. The gurita's face filled the screen, eyes wide when he saw her instead of his friend. "Someone's taken Uri," she said. "I need to get him back. Which means I need to know everything about the thing that took him."

"You guys can't ever ask me for anything easy, can you?"

"Easy is boring."

"Good point." She listened to the clicks of Vani's keyboard, almost taking comfort in the sound. Minutes passed before he spoke again. "Can you tell me anything about your new buddy?"

She shook her head. "It's...big. Taller than Uri, extremely fast. Big eyes. Slit, yellow eyes. From what I saw, his face and hands are covered in orange fur. Has claws, I think."

"Probably prone to chasing lasers, too."

"What?"

Vani grinned. "Earth joke, princess." After a few more clicks, an image filled the screen. "That look like him?"

It did, though the coloration wasn't completely accurate, but it had a similar build, the same slit eyes and fangs. "Somewhat. What is it?"

"Uri used to tell me stories of these creatures on Earth called cats. Apparently everything on Earth is capable of killing you, but these things seemed to enjoy killing for the fun of it. You ever heard of a fahir?"

"No."

"Time for a history lesson. The fahir is what

happened when Earth scientists decided to be cute and let their cat overlords into space with them. As they colonized new planets, the animals adapted to the new climates and surroundings, and over time, they developed into the lovely fuzzballs we have now. And now, they're mostly bounty hunters or police, or both."

Shadi shivered. "These used to be Earth creatures?"

"The joys of evolution, my dear. Rumors floated around a while back claiming the cats had been used in experiments, which resulted in those things, but no one knows for sure."

"I just need to know how to find Uri. The...fahir...said Evirax had hired it."

"Then we need to hurry."

***

"Wake up, human."

A hard slap brought him back from whatever dark place his mind had been in. Uri glanced around, unsure of where he was at first, but then he remembered. No Shadi. Good.

Blood trickled from his busted lip, but he gave the cat a wide smile, which earned him another slap.

"Where's the girl?" the fahir asked.

"Long gone, by now." No doubt she'd done what she wanted to do all along—taken his ship to rescue her brother.

"I'll find her, and, when I do, I will make you watch what I do to her."

"You touch her," Uri said, "and I will skin you alive, Catgut."

"We'll see about that, slave."

For a moment, he rested his head against the cool metal behind him. With the shackles on his wrists, he couldn't help remembering the day his own brother sold him to the Welles' group. Their ship had been something like this one, small but difficult to track, perfect for their original purpose of looting and killing. They must have gotten the ship Shadi grew up on much later.

Rather than wallow, he searched for a way to free his arms, but the ground around him was cleaner than he'd anticipated. *Balls. Luck favors the brave, not the stupid.* He'd have to bide his time, wait for the right opportunity.

After a while, the ship slowed and came to a stop. From the stench filling the room, he figured they needed to refuel. The hangar door opened—the only indication the fahir had left at all—and Uri forced himself to his feet. The change in position caused blood to rush to his head; his vision went black at the edges, but he had to do something. A fueling station wasn't his most ideal place to escape. Desperate times and all. He'd find plenty of hiding places, and he'd be able to hop a ship to the nearest Embassy from here. First, he had to get these chains off.

Too soon, the door opened again, and he hadn't found a damn thing to help. When his cell door creaked, he turned to face the fahir, maybe fight his way out. "Shadi?" She stood in the entryway, a laser cutter in one hand and in the other.... "Is that the drive core?"

With a grin, she cut the shackles off his wrists with expert precision. "It'll be harder for him to follow us with this missing." Her face and hands were covered in oil and grease, much like the first day he'd laid eyes on her.

"How did you...?"

"I'll explain once we get back to our ship."

Our ship. As they struggled back toward *Gemini*, she managed to support his weight. They wove

51

through crowds of merchants and drunks, somehow managing to stay undetected, and Uri still fought his disbelief. The thought that he was hallucinating crossed his mind more than once.

She settled him in the copilot's chair and took the helm, looking every bit as confident as someone who'd been flying for years. Without a hitch, she disengaged them from the station and into the relative safety of the stars. "You're amazing."

She smiled, and light pink blossomed in her cheeks. "Time to take care of you," she said. "Come on." Her slight frame contained hidden strength, and, regardless of the throbbing behind his eyes, he wanted her to stay this close. "Now, sit."

"You didn't have to come back." As instructed, he sat on the side of his bed while she fetched first-aid supplies. When she returned, she sat next to him, her knee against his.

"You'd have done it for me without a second thought." She dabbed at a cut above his eyebrow. "How's your head?"

"Hurts," he replied with a little snort. "But it's been worse. And you haven't answered my question."

Her attention moved to his split lip. As she dabbed at the cut, he noticed her fingers trembling, her hand unsteady. Could have been from the adrenaline. "Well, since you decided to get abducted, I contacted Vani. Learned a few things about Earth cats and the fahir, and about how to track ships. As an added bonus, he taught me how to disable our tracking signal."

"Which is illegal."

"Nothing we've done is legal. What's one more?" She scooted behind him. "You've got a knot the size of my fist back here. There has to be a compress on this ship somewhere. Vani apparently had it fitted for every conceivable human emergency."

"Like I told you. Worriers."

"Let me go find it. You could really use it."

Already, the improved nutrition she'd received over the last several weeks had made a difference. Her waist-length hair bounced with each step she took, and her eyes were brighter, keener. And the sway of her hips certainly caught his attention. She wasn't the waif he'd stolen from Goliv. Somewhere along the way, she'd become a woman.

A woman who'd risked herself to save him.

When she came back, he noted the grace in each movement, from the way she walked to the way she handed him the compress and sat next to him. "Why did you return for me?"

The gentleness of her fingertips on his cheek managed to cut through the horrible pain in his head. "I had to. You promised to help me. Can't keep your promises if you're in the forge." She kissed the uninjured side of his mouth, and his heart sprinted into high gear. "Besides, what kind of wife would I be if I left my dear husband to rot?"

"In my experience, a happy one." He took a chance, cupped her cheek with his palm, and, to his amazement, she leaned into his touch. For the first time, he noticed the flecks of amber in her irises and the light freckles on her skin. Then she kissed him again, and he pulled her tight, desperate to feel her body pressed to his. He tangled one hand in her long hair and moved the other to rest on her hip. All the pain in the universe couldn't strip this pleasure from him.

When she pulled away, she smiled and blushed and curled into him, resting her head on his shoulder. "I can't do this without you. I *won't* do this without you."

"Good. Because I won't let you. I mean what I said, Shadi. I'll help you find Shilah."

"I know. We just need a place to start."

Chapter Thirteen

Shadi forced him to get some rest, though, after that kiss, sleep did not come easily. He lay in bed, staring at the ceiling, compress against the knot the fahir gave him. She couldn't shoot, but she had her own ways to protect herself. Clever, clever girl.

Eventually, the ship lulled him into a fitful sleep and, when he woke, the ache had subsided some. With a bit of effort, he pushed himself up and, after the head rush subsided, headed toward the cockpit where Shadi sat, staring through the window. She didn't budge when he took the other chair.

For a while, he rested in contented silence with her while she worked out whatever was going through her mind. Her face never changed, except for an occasional crinkling of her eyes, as though what she thought about caused her pain. Then she finally reached toward him without looking away from the stars, and he grasped her cold hand in his. "You're up sooner than I expected," she said

"Stubborn, you know. Sleep and I are not the best of friends, anyway."

She chuckled. "Are you feeling better?"

"Now," he said, giving her fingers a gentle squeeze. "What had you so deep in thought?"

"Shilah." Her brother's name barely a whisper, as though all of her hope had been carried away. "I'm...scared. Vani's been searching, and so have I, and we haven't found anything yet."

"We will. I made you a promise."

"You did." She shifted in the chair, drew her knees against her chest, but still refused to let go of his hand.

"The nyx only have so many colonies. If we must, we'll search them all, one by one, until we find your brother. I'll not let Evirax claim another human."

Finally, she looked at him, a sea of questions filling her beautiful green eyes. Instead of asking anything, she turned back to the console. "You lost someone to them."

"I did. She wouldn't have been special had she not been the only other human I had contact with. The nyx purchased us both around the same time. Then they worked her to death."

He'd never forget the day Gabby died. Evirax had been particularly vicious that day, pushing every slave to his breaking point. Covered in sweat and soot, Uri worked until his fingers blistered, until dehydration and exhaustion threatened to claim him, but Gabby fell first.

"It was brutal," he said. "She tried to work through it, but she swayed and collapsed. Her head hit the side of the forge at the perfect angle. She died on the spot, and all they did was take her body past the outskirts of camp and leave her for the wild animals to deal with." He closed his eyes, concentrating on the feel of Shadi's hand in his. "The day I saw you, I saw her. You're stronger, I can tell, but I wouldn't take the risk."

"Uri...."

The console beeped. A message from Vani, perhaps?

After a moment's hesitation, Shadi pushed the blinking green button. The gurita's face filled the screen. "Found something."

They passed a look. This might be it.

"Tarbos. Home of one of the largest taralsite mines in the galaxy." Vani paused. "Rumor has it they've got a human foreman."

"Shilah," she breathed. The look of hope on her

56

face nearly broke Uri's heart. "But a foreman? What does that mean?"

Uri sighed. "It means he's like Evirax."

Not Shilah. When they were children, he'd never been anything less than a kind, gentle-hearted boy. The idea of him hurting slaves soured her stomach. She released Uri's hand, almost wincing at the broken connection, and headed back toward the bedroom she'd claimed, the one in which she'd kissed her abductor, her protector, her...what? Clutching her stomach, she reached the bathroom and fell to her knees in front of the toilet, where she emptied out everything—her grief, her despair, her hope her brother had somehow lasted the last several years unscathed, that he'd be the same boy she remembered when they reunited. Tears burned her eyes. Her head throbbed. This wasn't the news she'd wanted.

Once she crawled out of the bathroom, she curled into a ball on the bedroom floor, imagining her brother's brutality. Had he become the same kind of monster as Evirax? Or something worse?

Pull it together. For all she knew, he'd been forced into this. Or it was someone else. It had to be someone else. *Please. Please be someone else....*

***

They had a bit of preparation work to do before they could even think about approaching Tarbos. Landing on a nyx-colony planet by accident was one thing, but to land on one on purpose while plotting to steal not just a slave but a foreman? Uri wondered if he'd lost his mind, especially considering Evirax had hired a bounty hunter to pursue him—and fahir were *not* easily dissuaded—but then he'd glance at Shadi and his purpose would be renewed.

"We'll have to stop for supplies," he said, "and to repair the ship. There's a safe place to port on Chanterelle. We'll be scanned again, but with the new identifications, we at least won't be chased again."

She nodded. "They'll think I'm Leida."

"Yes."

"And then Judah will find out. Come after us."

"We'll be ready, Shadi." He hoped, anyway. "They won't take you."

"What about you?" she asked so quietly he almost thought he'd imagined her question.

"Me? What of me?"

"You're in the same situation I am. An escaped slave, former property of the nyx. Evirax put a bounty out on you. Face it: If the Welles' group finds us, or if that fahir finds us, we're screwed."

"First of all, Evirax was giving Catgut a bonus. The bounty is on you."

With a huff, she said, "Doesn't matter. The giant cat is after us both."

"Second," he continued, "Welles won't find us. They're nowhere near this sector, and if for some reason they do get a blip concerning Leida's whereabouts, we'll be off-planet long before they arrive."

Shadi stayed quiet for a time, seemingly weighing the truth of his words while he prayed they *would* be true. A bounty hunter presented enough issues. The involvement of Judah Welles complicated matters to a point he couldn't even fathom. "Would you kill him?"

"Who? Judah?"

She nodded once.

"I will do whatever I must to keep you safe."

"Why? To alleviate your guilt from some girl dying in the forge?"

"No. Because I made you a promise." What else did she want him to say?

"Your promises mean that much to you."

"More than anything."

"They're only words, Uri. Words change nothing."

"Sometimes, words are all a man has. Promises, vows, oaths. These keep a man honest, focused, driven. I strive to be a keeper of my words." Unable to sit any longer, he stood and paced the length of the cockpit, which allowed him just enough room to work off a bit of his nervous energy. Even with all his talk of honesty, he couldn't tell her why it was so important Judah Welles believe his sister to be alive.

The vow he'd made the day they attacked his colony never left him, and he intended to see it completed.

He would kill Ezra Welles.

Chapter Fourteen

Shadi forced herself to sleep. After spending so much time worrying and fearing for Uri, talking to Vani, and having her hope toyed with, she needed to lie down. Decompress. Nothing made sense anymore, not even her own actions. Why had she kissed Uri?

Yes, she'd grown to care about him, but to make any kind of physical connection was a bad idea. Horrible. Stupid. Amazing. Wonderful. Unlike anything she'd ever experienced. No. She needed to find Shilah, get him to a safe place. Her loyalty had to stay with her brother, no matter the possibilities Uri held. No matter the temptation to pursue something she had no way of understanding or the strange way her stomach reacted to his presence, or how her hands shook when she recalled the kiss.

What a mess. Before, she'd never had a chance to connect with someone else, aside from her brother and Ezra, though those memories were ruined. Never needed to. She did her work in the forge like a good slave, ate her *meals* alone, slept alone. None of the other aliens ever approached her—even the nyx stayed away—and she finally knew why. They feared her for reasons she knew nothing about.

Reasons she planned to exploit. Though the fahir seemed unaffected by the rumors and stories Uri had told her, others weren't. If need be, she'd embody all of those fears—her favorites being that humans were born out of fire and that they had tournaments where they had to fight to the death just for the amusement of the upper classes. Anything to get her brother back and keep Uri from the forge, or worse. Evirax's sadistic side had no end. She'd seen him gun down slaves in cold blood.

For the next several hours, she racked her brain for every bit of information Ezra had ever told her about his daughter. If she had any hope of pulling this off, she had to become Leida. The nyx could not know she'd had escaped one of their colonies.

She'd never seen a picture of the woman, didn't know her age, either, but Vani had selected this ID for a reason, so surely they shared some resemblance, and they must have been reasonably close in age.

From what she recalled of Ezra's stories, Leida had been take-charge—which explained why the gurita at the dealership had deferred to her—and intimidating like her father. Most of the time, Ezra's kindness colored every interaction, but she'd witnessed his stone-cold demeanor with other slaves. When his eyes turned icy and he set his mouth in a harsh line, the man personified intimidation.

And, apparently, his daughter was cut from the same cloth.

I can do this, she told herself. *I can play the part until Shilah is safe.*

While Shadi rested, Uri palmed the hilt of a dagger he'd stolen from a pirate three years prior. Constructed of ivory, the hilt curved to fit his palm perfectly, with small ridges carved into the bone to help with the grip. The blade needed sharpening, but he could take care of that with no difficulty.

The day he saw the dagger, he almost hadn't recognized it, though it'd sat atop his mother's bookcase since he'd been alive. In a run-down bar on some back-water colony he no longer remembered the name of, he'd spotted an urok surrounded by a crowd of onlookers, telling some half-baked story of how it'd killed a human to take this amazing dagger for itself. Uri called bullshit, shot the alien in the head, and reclaimed the family heirloom stolen by Ezra Welles so long ago.

The dagger he intended to kill his brother with.

By right as eldest, William had claim to the dagger, but he hadn't wanted it and had given it, as well as everything else, to Ezra Welles the day they stormed the colony. This knife was all they had left from when their family lived on Earth, before everything went to hell. Shadi would never know about it; she was too young. But he remembered the old days, when life got so bad that only on the clearest nights, which were few and far between, did he spot the blinking lights of the colony's construction. On occasion, he saw an outline of the new station, like a fading dream. Staring into the sky, he'd never believed the dream to be a nightmare, but it was.

The console beeped and drew him back to the present. Expecting Vani, he pressed the button. The face filling his screen nearly had him falling out of his chair. "Not very smart, are you?" the fahir asked.

Uri stared at the bounty hunter, hand still clutching the dagger. "You're the one who lost his drive core, Catgut." Offering what he hoped to be a lackadaisical grin, in his mind, he asked himself how the cat had found the ship's comm channel when Shadi had disabled the signal.

The fahir growled at the insult. "Your bitch will get her due, I assure you."

"I'll kill you first."

"You did so great last time we met. I look forward to you trying again." Pulling back its lips in a feral sneer, the fahir said, "I will find you, and I will force you to watch me pick her apart, piece by piece, until there's nothing left but bone and blood." Then it cut the comm link, leaving Uri's heart lodged in his throat.

Before he dealt with William, he needed to make certain this damned fahir couldn't follow. And he knew exactly who to speak with for ideas.

Chapter Fifteen

A knock on the door startled her, and she forgot her train of thought. Ezra had told her and Shilah about Leida and how she liked to play pranks on her brother and cousins. Most of the time, they were harmless, but once.... And that's where she lost the story. Grumbling, she let Uri in. The look on his face quieted any bit of snark in her throat. "What's wrong?"

"The fahir," he ground out. "Somehow it found our comm signal."

"Doesn't mean it'll find us."

"No, but it will try. Fahir do not give up, no matter what. I'm sure Evirax's bounty alone is enough to keep it tracking us, but since you rescued me and stole its drive core, the hunt has become personal."

So she'd made her first true enemy. For some reason, the idea excited her. "What do you suggest?"

Taking a seat on the edge of the bed, he rested an ankle on the opposite knee and looked at her with beautiful brown eyes sparkling. "How much do you know about Catgut's ship?"

She shrugged. During her time on Goliv, she'd worked on dozens, maybe hundreds, of ships. Judah had taught her how ships worked after seeing her interest in them. Maybe he thought a slave with electronics knowledge would fetch a better price. Regardless, it was the only thing she'd learned from him. "It's not that special," she replied. "Class-IV cruiser. A few upgrades to the shields and mounted front guns. The drive core was simple to remove." Crossing her arms over her chest, she asked, "What

64

are you plotting?"

"A bit of sabotage."

"Fatal?"

"Possibly."

After a few seconds, she nodded. "I think I know what to do."

***

Shadi tightened the buckle of her boot and then stood to check her reflection. On Dalara, she'd paid attention to how women dressed and carried themselves and hoped to mimic what she'd seen. The clothes Vani had provided fit better since she'd put on weight, and her hair was clean and shiny, with a small wave. Surely she'd pass for a Welles.

When she rejoined her companion, he gave her a look that shot fire through her veins, and she thought about their kiss again. Next time, she wanted more. To touch him, feel him touch her. It'd have to wait. "Is this okay?" she asked.

"Perfect, except...." He reached into his pocket. "You're missing something." Opening his hand, he revealed her ring. By this point, she'd forgotten about the blasted thing. She moved to take it, but he took her hand and slipped the ring onto the appropriate finger, holding her gaze the entire time. "There," his voice low. "Now you're perfect."

So are you. Without hesitating, she leaned in to kiss him. He wrapped her in his arms, pulled her tight so that she felt every defined muscle beneath his clothes. Her instincts had her untucking his shirt to feel his skin, but he broke away and grabbed her wrists.

"Soon," he said. "Just...not yet."

"Right." Duty first. The fahir. They had to deal with the fahir.

"Are you prepared for this?"

"My part's easy. I'm more concerned for you."

He smoothed her hair. "Don't be. I made you a promise."

"And you always keep your word," she said with a smile. "So might I ask you for one more?"

"Certainly."

"Promise me you won't do anything stupid."

With a sad smile, he kissed her forehead and left.

***

He wanted to promise, but he planned to end this damned cat one way or another. Her safety mattered more than his own. Something he never thought possible, but this crazy adventure proved to be full of surprises. While they waited for the scanner drones, she smiled at him, and he knew in that moment he had to do everything possible to keep her from getting hurt.

After a successful scan, they exited the ship and waited in a nearby alcove. The moment she saw the fahir's cruiser, Shadi gave him a peck on the cheek and hid in a different location where she'd still be able to see him. By his figuring, the bounty hunter would want Shadi first. He planned to be a worthwhile distraction, give her time to disable the ship, though he didn't know how much time she'd need. After all these years, he had to worry about another person. The emotion was strangely liberating.

Then he spotted the fahir. Pressing himself against the alcove wall, he observed for a few moments, taking note of the two guns strapped to either side of the cat's body. Two guns? He'd faced worse odds.

As long as he kept the thing away from Shadi,

this would be fine.

"Hey, Catgut." He stepped out of the shadows, a wide smile on his face, like he and the cat were good friends. It narrowed its eyes, clawed hand hovering above one of its guns, and then thought better of it.

"Well, well. Coming to give yourself up?"

Uri snorted. "No, no, not in the least. I've come to make you an offer."

The magic word. "You can't offer me anything Evirax can't."

"I can offer you something he *won't*."

"Which is?"

Think fast, think fast, think fast. "An alternative." Uri turned and headed toward the more heavily populated areas, where, in theory, the fahir wouldn't shoot. He waited for Catgut to follow before starting the biggest bluff of his life. "A cat taking orders from a fish. Don't you see the irony?"

A low growl was the reply.

"What do you know about Earth history?" *Jesus, what are you doing?*

"Not much."

"In ancient Egypt, cats were treated like royalty. They were practically gods, buried with pharaohs. Now look what you're reduced to. A scavenger. Getting scraps from the blowfish when you can." With a harsh laugh, he said, "You're pathetic."

As he expected, the fahir didn't take kindly to the insult. Its massive hand landed on Uri's shoulder hard enough to make him stumble. To keep him from falling, it grabbed his shirt and forced him to look at it. "Keep talking like that, and you'll be a dead human."

"I'm only stating the truth." *Any time you want to contact me, Shadi....*

***

The moment Uri walked away with the bounty hunter, she sprang into action. Evading the guards, she crept to the cruiser, popped the lock, and disappeared inside.

Glancing at the condition of the ship, she wondered how the creature had done so well with such a ratty vessel. The guns had to be the only upgrade it'd gotten since its purchasing. She shook her head. Judah would have been appalled.

Without any more hesitation, she went to work. Uri was out there with that thing. Best to hurry.

Draining the shields took the most time, and the trick would be in resetting the gauge to full capacity. She opened the cover and tinkered with the wiring. One simple, preventable malfunction—had the cat upgraded its console. *Tsk, tsk.*

Once she completed the rewiring and replaced the panel, she had to wait, make sure everything went as planned. A few tense minutes passed, and then a few more. She checked for something else to sabotage, anything to make their escape easier, but short of removing the drive core again, she had nothing else to do.

Just...wait.

Chapter Sixteen

Enough time passed that Shadi left the fahir's ship with confidence. She tried to contact Uri, but Chanterelle's high magnetic field blocked the comm signal. Time to find him the old-fashioned way.

She headed in the same direction he'd led the cat. A common area lay in front of her, a series of shops lining either side of the narrow street. Safety in a crowd. Smart.

Scanning the area, she saw no sign of Uri or their furry friend.

Her heart slammed into overdrive. With adrenaline flooding her system, she started to panic. What if he'd done something stupid after all? And he would, she knew. He'd do it for her. "Dammit," she muttered. She'd traverse every street, check every shop and alleyway to find him. "I'm not leaving here without you."

The shops didn't help. None of the shopkeepers had seen a human and fahir. She followed the road until it ended at a sandy expanse leading to what looked like a large drop. Two sets of footprints marred the pathway.

What have you done? If the fahir hadn't killed him, she'd do it for making her worry.

"Oliver?" she called, knowing they needed to keep up appearances. No reply. She cursed again. Where had he gone? Some husband he was turning out to be.

Swallowing her fear, she peeked over the side of the cliff, but she couldn't see anything for the darkness. She tried the comm one more time. Nothing. Not even static.

Maybe I should go wait at the ship. By that point, *Gemini*'s engines had cooled too much to ensure a proper takeoff. Uri had to be okay. He had no other choice.

Then, she heard the footsteps behind her. Relief flooded her system, forcing her down from her adrenaline high. "There you are," she said as she turned around. But she stopped short. Uri wasn't waiting for her.

His white hair had grown shaggy, almost down to his shoulders, and he had more wrinkles than she remembered, but right in front of her stood Ezra Welles.

Backlit by the streetlights, he looked like a specter from her past. Instinct drew her away from him—he *had* sold her, after all—and yet she wanted nothing more than his arms around her. Flashes from her childhood filled her mind, a kaleidoscope of memories good and bad.

A sense of betrayal slithered through her veins. As he approached, she stood her ground. He stopped about a foot away, blue eyes crinkled. "You...you're not Leida." Reaching behind him, he revealed the pistol he'd taught Shilah to shoot. "Who the hell are you?"

Tears filled Shadi's eyes. "A girl you sold a long time ago."

Understanding softened his features. "Holy God above," he said, reaching out to her, "Shadi."

She felt like a child again. Remembered Ezra packing her through the ship's corridors, playing stupid games with her, letting her know he loved her. "How could you?" she asked. His calloused fingertips wiped away her tears. "I loved you and you...."

"I know, kid. I know." She let him pull her into a hug, but she stood there like a block of ice, wishing his warmth could melt her and she might love him again. Everything Uri had told her filled her mind, and a sob broke through.

"Shilah's gone." The words were muffled by his shirt, but by the way he stiffened, he heard her.

"What do you mean?"

Pulling away to wipe her eyes, she hesitated. Why bother? Ezra stood in front of her. Ezra, her friend, her father, her confidante. "The nyx moved him to another colony. Years ago."

He scrubbed a hand over his face. "Goddamn it. One of the conditions was that Evirax not separate you."

"It did. I think he's on another colony, but I don't know for sure." Panic welled up in her again. "I need to find him, Ezra." *But I need to find Uri first.*

With a gentleness most didn't know he was capable of, Ezra led her to a nearby bench. "Tell me everything."

Without hesitation, she did. When she finished, he sat silent for a moment. "I'd heard about that, too. Judah's back on human trade."

"So...."

"Probably ain't him, kid. I'm sorry." He huffed. "I can't believe they separated you."

Me, neither. "There goes our only lead. According to our source, the human's a foreman."

He cocked an eyebrow. "'Our'?"

Balls. "I didn't escape on my own. I had help."

"So you're out here with somebody. Good," he said to himself, "that's real good."

"Someone who knows you."

Shadi nearly jumped out of her skin. Lost in her conversation, she didn't hear anyone approach. Behind the bench stood Uri, bloodied, with clothes ripped. A large gash covered his chest. He held his blaster to Ezra's head.

Uri grunted. "I've waited a long time for this."

Torn between love and loyalty, Shadi watched her companion's finger, waiting for him to pull the trigger. He'd earned this, and Ezra had brought it upon himself. Still, she feared this side of Uri. "Don't," she whispered.

He met her gaze and lowered the gun, resignation all over his face. "You're lucky she loves you," he practically growled. "I ought to kill you on the spot and damn the consequences."

"Nobody'd blame you for it, or miss me." Ezra stood and faced his would-be murderer. The two eyed each other for several long minutes. "I remember you. Scrappy thing when you were little." He took a deep breath. "Glad to see you made it."

***

Uri had no idea what to say. After spending years dreaming of the day he thanked Ezra Welles for turning his life into hell, he never expected to stay his hand or to hear the slaver say anything like that. He swallowed against the lump in his throat. "Thank you."

A quick glance at Shadi showed him a woman relieved. Though she still chewed her bottom lip, the tightness around her eyes had left. Killing Welles wasn't worth Shadi's hatred.

He ran his fingers through her hair and smiled when she leaned into his touch. "I guess now the question is, can you help us find Shilah?"

"Probably ought to do something about those wounds first."

He bristled. "You have no right or reason to be concerned for me. Answer my question."

Welles shook his head. "I wouldn't have a way to find anything."

"One of the most well-connected men in the

galaxy, and you can't help us? Or *won't* help us?"

Welles sighed and seemed to age another fifty years. "Look, I've spent a lot of my life regretting what happened at New Eden. That place was a shit hole anyway. You didn't need my crew coming in there and fucking it all up for you." A hard glint entered the old man's eyes, and Uri dreaded the next words. For a moment, he imagined himself at five years old, staring up at young Ezra Welles while William, twelve at the time, brokered a trade. "We were desperate."

"I don't want to hear your pitiful story." Uri pulled away from Shadi and considered raising his gun again.

"You're going to. Because I'm tired of living with this damn guilt." He took a breath. "We were out of work. Judah had just been born and I had to find a way to feed him. The raids were keeping us alive— barely—but we needed more. When your brother suggested...."

"William is of no consequence now." *If ever he was.*

"Wait," Shadi said. "Just wait. William? *Liam* is your brother?"

"Apparently so."

"Heh. You never could say his whole name. Shilah always called him Will, but you liked Liam better." Ezra shook his head. "It's all fucked up."

"No shit," she muttered. "You...this whole time I thought you were going to rescue me and Shilah. That we were going to be a family. You never planned on it, did you?" She made a disgusted noise and stood. "I should've known better. Can you at least tell me why?"

"I ain't got a good reason." For the first time, the old man dropped his gaze. "The day we dropped you off, I was drunker'n I'd ever been. I barely remember telling you good-bye."

Shadi's eyes went wide, and tears threatened to spill at any moment. Uri tried to rest his hand on her shoulder again, offer some small comfort, but she shook him off and stood on shaking legs. "I have spent the entirety of my life waiting. Waiting for you to come back. Waiting for you so we could find Shilah and have the stupid life you *promised* me we'd have, and you mean to tell me it was all a lie because you couldn't remember?" She was almost screaming. Passersby stopped to stare. "Because you were *drunk*?"

"I'm sorry, kid...."

"That isn't good enough!" She sat again, trembling, and Uri had no way to help her.

Kneeling in front of her, Ezra took her limp hands in his, but she didn't look at him, just the ground. "If I'd known, if I'd remembered, I would've. I loved you kids like my own. Better'n my own. I wouldn't have let the deal go through if I didn't have to."

"But you had to," she muttered.

"I did. I'm sorry, Shadi."

She jerked her hands from his and pulled her knees to her chest. "Your apologies are worthless."

"'Cuz he's a worthless old man.

Looking past Ezra, Uri raised his gun again. The new voice belonged to a man a couple inches taller than Welles, with the same ice-blue eyes and scowl. Judah.

Holy shit. If he took them both out, right here, the largest slaver ring in the galaxy would crumble. To his surprise, the younger Welles trained his gun on his father.

"What are you doin' here, boy?"

"Heard Leida'd popped up. Came to see if it was true." He looked to Shadi. "Guess not."

She stood, defiant, chin held high. Tears no longer threatened her eyes.

"You might want to get out of here, miss. This is about to get ugly."

"You don't recognize her, do you, boy?" Shifting toward his son, Ezra tensed. "You taught that girl everything she knows."

Was the old man hoping for a family reunion? If so, Judah didn't look as happy to see her as he'd probably hoped.

The younger Welles snorted. "You're still alive. I'm impressed."

"No thanks to you."

"Give me one good reason not to pull the trigger," Uri said.

"Oh, you." Dark amusement filled his eyes. "I remember you now. Your brother got a hell of a reward for sending you my way."

"He deserved a bullet to the head. Nothing more."

"That why you're gonna shoot me? Because William handed you over?"

Gun still trained on Judah, Uri stepped around the bench. "Get her back to our ship," he whispered to Ezra. The old man nodded.

"Hell no. You're not going anywhere, Dad."

Before Uri reacted, Judah fired.

"Shadi!" As Ezra crumpled to the ground, Uri blocked her from the sight as best he could. She trembled against him, breath coming in harsh gasps.

Judah trained his gun on them. "I can't believe either of you survived the nyx."

Without a second thought, Uri turned and shot.

Chapter Seventeen

Ezra had always said Judah would be the one to kill him.

Sometimes when he'd had too much to drink, he'd mention it, how his boy had become cold, calculating, cruel, while Leida had been a kind, sweet child. He'd tell her that she reminded him of his daughter, how much he missed her.

Now he was dead. The few memories she had of him tainted, worthless. Useless. She hated knowing that the man she'd loved so fervently had never existed. That she'd given her hope, her affection, her salvation to a man who couldn't even remember he'd made a promise; even if he had remembered it, she doubted he'd meant it.

If only she could have gotten help finding Shilah.... Though Ezra claimed he had no way to help, Judah might have known something. Instead, she had less than nothing, and her determination to find her brother had all but disappeared.

Uri half carried her back to *Gemini* while she fought back sobs, unable to wipe the tears from her eyes. Two bodies lay in heaps behind them, two pieces of what little life she'd thought she had...gone. Revealed to be lies. Once they were back on the ship, life resumed its normalcy. Being near the console she'd grown so familiar with helped ease her. She had duties. Uri needed tending to. As far as she knew, they still had the fahir to deal with, though, judging from the gashes on his chest....

"What happened with Catgut?" she asked, not sure she wanted to hear the answer.

"Incapacitated for the moment, but he'll be after

us." His voice lacked its usual depth and strength. "I take it everything went well with the shields?"

"Perfect," she managed. "He won't be able to follow. The first bit of space dust will take him out." Settling him in the captain's chair, she retrieved the first aid kit.

"When we're off-world." He managed a weak smile. "The scratches look far worse than they are."

She nodded. But a question refused to stop rolling in her mind. "Is Judah dead?"

He detected a hint of hope that both crushed and elated him. He'd feared her reaction to shooting Judah, but not enough to let it deter him. Her safety mattered to him far more than the life of either Welles. If she didn't hate him for protecting her, all the better.

"Truthfully, I don't know. I didn't stop to check for a pulse."

She nodded, eyes red and swollen. "I hope so," she said, her voice cracking. "I saw the way he looked at you, like you were *nothing* and all I could think was, 'I hope Uri shoots him.' *I* wanted to shoot him." She took a shaky breath. "Am I a bad person?"

"No."

He remained quiet while *Gemini* struggled against Chanterelle's gravitational pull. Once they were safely nestled among the stars, he turned back to her. "Judah Welles was scum. He certainly didn't deserve your sympathy. I...am sorry about Ezra, though."

"Don't be. He didn't deserve your forgiveness." She popped open the med kit and started pulling out a slew of supplies, operating on autopilot. As she worked, he noted the faraway look glazing her eyes and the way her hands still shook. After she applied the antibiotic ointment, she stopped and took a deep breath, and when she looked at him again, it was with resignation. "At this point, I care about two people: Shilah, and you. The rest don't matter."

After she patched him up, she curled in the copilot's chair, hugging her legs to her chest, staring blankly into space. He wished for a way to help her forget the trauma, but how?

"Shadi, we're safe for now. We need to clean up, try to sleep."

"The bed is too soft," she mumbled against her knee.

"How about we make a bed in the floor, then?"

Barely, she nodded. Ensuring the autopilot accepted the coordinates, he took her hand and led her to the back, where she'd been sleeping on the floor anyway. He rummaged through the rest of the clothing Vani had purchased for her and found a suitable nightgown. Nothing fancy, but soft and comfortable, what she needed. After she fell asleep, he'd incinerate their clothing. No need to leave reminders behind.

Without speaking, he led her into the bathroom. She still trembled, though it'd subsided some. Ezra's blood covered her shirt. Regardless of the pain flaring in his chest with each movement, he arranged her gown and turned on the water. "I'm sorry," she whispered.

The look on her face broke his heart. Her wide eyes were rimmed with tears. "For what?"

"You wouldn't have to deal with all this if not for me."

He kissed her lightly on the temple, smoothed her hair. "You are by far the best decision I've ever made. No regrets."

She didn't speak again for a minute or two, instead considering his words with a furrowed brow and pursed lips. Unable to resist, he leaned down to kiss her, intending a soft, simple one to calm her. Instead, she opened her mouth to him, an explosive passion brimming just beneath the surface.

Her fingertips danced along his rib cage, every brush of her skin against his igniting a fire in his blood. God, he needed her. So badly. The universe was on the verge of going to shit, had been shit for a long time. One good thing.... All he wanted was one good thing, and he had it with her, a girl he'd rescued on impulse, had intended to deliver to the Embassy, and could not let go of, no matter how he thought he should.

As her hands explored his shoulders and back, he let his drift down her cheek and along her jawline, to her soft neck and the swell of her breasts. Slow, tender touches that would allow her to stay his hand if she needed him to stop. And no matter how he wanted her, he'd stop if she asked.

Lost in her, he took time and satisfaction in touching her, learning her body through her clothing. Across her stomach and then down her thigh, each muscle tensing and relaxing beneath his hand. He longed to kiss her along that trail, to listen to her soft moans and whimpers, to pleasure her, help her forget this horrific day. The pain from his wounds faded to nothing. All he knew was her.

In all his years, he'd never loved another soul. His time in the forge had hardened him, and yet she broke his defenses without effort.

Unwillingly, he broke away from her. "Your water will get cold."

"Join me?"

How could he resist?

Forcing himself to take his time, he unbuttoned her ruined blouse with trembling, fumbling fingers, savoring each inch of creamy flesh revealed. Throat dry, he slipped it off her shoulders, and she let it fall to the floor. She was still a little thin but in a way that suited her, with small breasts and a slightly rounded tummy that spoke of her improving health. "Have a seat," his voice strained. "Your boots need to come off."

She complied. He tugged off her boots and thick wool socks and pulled her back to her feet. "Trousers, next." With slow, deliberate movements, he uncinched the belt and pulled it through the loops. "If you want me to stop, you say the word."

"I will."

Once he'd divested her of her clothing, he took everything and piled the bundle in the corner to be dealt with later. When he turned back to her, she smiled, and though it didn't quite reach her eyes, he'd take it. "Your turn," she said so softly he almost didn't hear her.

"You don't have to, love. I can take care of myself."

"I want to."

Words he never thought he'd hear her say, though the inflection lacked warmth but not desire. After she'd nearly escaped at the fuel station, after telling her the truth about Ezra on Dalara.... He had no idea how they'd gotten this far, but he'd be damned if he screwed it up, especially when she had to be in shock from what happened. Hell, *he* was in shock, but he hadn't just suffered the great loss she had. Time and gentleness would get her through this.

She reached for him and held him close. The feel of her skin against his chest was a heaven he never wanted to leave. As she worked on his trousers, he savored each brush of her fingertips against his stomach. In moments, they stood naked together. This was all new for her. So long without any of her kind, she had to be operating on pure instinct. As badly as he wanted her, he needed to be patient, let her explore, no matter the agony it might cause him.

He helped her into the shower, and the hot water sluicing over their bodies washed away some of the day's stress. Grabbing the bottle of soap, he squeezed some into his palm and smoothed it over her back, around her stomach, and up to her breasts. With a soft whimper, she leaned against him, wrapping her arms around his neck. "Let me take care of you."

"You always do."

"This time, I've something different in mind." Hands on her hips, he turned her to face him. She dipped her head back to keep the water from her eyes, and in that moment, he knew no better perfection than her. He kissed the smooth column of her neck, her shoulders, collarbones, whatever he reached with ease. As he continued his ministrations, her breathing deepened. Perfect.

He sank to his knees, pressed his lips to her stomach, her hips, her thighs. Couldn't get enough of her soft skin. And when he tasted her.... His moan matched hers.

"Uri," she breathed. "Don't stop."

Never. While he ran his tongue, slowly, languidly, from her opening to her clitoris, he stroked the inside of her thigh with one hand and held her steady with the other. It wouldn't take long for her to come, and he couldn't wait to hear her.

For a moment, he pulled away, and the sheer lust blazing in her eyes stripped away the last bits of his self-control. "If this gets too intense, and you need me to stop," he said, "tell me. Please."

"Mmm-hmm."

He slipped a finger inside her, gave her a chance to adjust to the pressure. After all, he didn't want to hurt her. Though he knew she wasn't breakable or a delicate flower—no one left the forge unscathed—he wanted her to enjoy this. From the way she whimpered.... So far, so good. He swirled his tongue around her clitoris, lightly pulled it into his mouth. Her hips jerked, and the resulting gasp made him so hard, his balls ached.

"Uri...."

"You're okay, love. I have you. Let go."

Digging her nails into his shoulder, she shuddered. Her inner muscles spasmed around his finger, and her whimpers and cries filled his ears with music more beautiful than any he'd ever heard. After she climaxed, she braced herself against him; he gripped her hips and stood to let her catch her breath. So beautiful, with her bright-green eyes heavy lidded and her pretty mouth slightly open. Her skin flushed light pink over her breasts and her neck. She nuzzled against his chest. "That was.... I...."

"Yes." He chuckled. "How do you feel?"

"Light." She glanced up at him. "I want more."

"Greedy."

"Maybe." As he reached behind her to shut off the water, she pressed her lips to his chest, above his heart. "I...love you. I think. I mean, I don't know for certain, but...but I can't imagine being without you anymore."

"And you won't be."

"Promise?"

"Promise."

Once they stepped out of the shower, Uri draped a towel around her before getting one for himself. She hadn't had a chance to learn his body the way he'd learned hers, but truly, she didn't know where to begin.

His back to her, she took the opportunity to trace the contours of his muscles, which flexed with every movement he made. Every inch of his dark skin beckoned to her, to be touched, to be caressed, kissed, licked. The white towel covering his waist drew her attention to his thighs and calves, which were covered in light scars. Probably from a lash. The nyx loved their archaic torture tools. But like the ones on his forearms, his chest, and his back, they only added to his allure. Proved his strength. And that a man with such a history managed to be so gentle, caring, and loving showed his character. Leaving Goliv with him hadn't been a mistake. It'd changed everything.

"I want to learn how to do...that...for you."

"There will be time." He caressed her cheek. "For now, we need to rest."

"No."

Amusement and shock flickered across his face. "No?"

"I'm not tired." Understatement. Though her body felt limp, like the noodles in the soup she and Uri had on Dalara, she was full of more excitement and energy than she ever had been. "I want more. I want...you."

"So do I." That *look* entered his eyes, the one he'd given her so many times before and she hadn't understood. He'd desired her this entire time, even when she'd been broken. The realization flooded her system with white-hot heat.

She wanted to give him everything she had to offer.

Uri threaded his fingers through her wet hair and pulled her flush against him, pressing his lips to hers with a kiss so searing she thought she'd burst into flames right then and there. His tongue pressed against the seam of her lips, and she opened to him without hesitation, lust and love and a thousand other things flowing through her blood. Being with him these last few weeks had opened her eyes to more than she'd ever thought possible, and this?

Though this frightened her, it brought her to life. Nothing to fear, everything to gain. She'd been mistaken when she'd thought she had less than nothing. She had him.

He lifted her in his arms and carried her to the makeshift bed in the floor. With the hardness of the floor beneath her and his hardness on top of her, she couldn't think of a better place to be.

"Are you certain this is what you want?"

"How many times are you going to ask? I'm not changing my mind."

"I don't want to hurt you."

Silly. She cupped his cheek. "You couldn't. I know that. I trust you." *I need you*.

He leaned in and kissed her palm. "Your faith in me is astounding."

"You haven't given me a reason to doubt. So don't start now."

His eyes brightened. "I'd never dream of it."

"Good." As she stroked his ribs, he removed his towel, keeping one hand tangled in her hair. Anticipation fluttered in her chest and between her thighs. She thought about his finger inside her, craved more than that. Fullness. Completeness. Whatever came next. "I'm ready."

Sitting back on his knees, he stroked himself a couple of times then positioned himself at her opening. "Tell me if it's too much."

"I can't tell you anything if you don't *do* anything," she teased.

One side of his mouth lifted in a grin. Then he slowly entered her. "Breathe, Shadi."

Right. She hadn't realized she held her breath. Through the discomfort, she managed a deep, even rhythm, which helped her adjust to the pressure. He kissed her again, soft and soothing. Yes, this was good. Exactly what she'd wanted.

After a few moments, he moved his hips—again, slowly, like he'd break her—and pressure already built in her core, like in the shower. She knew so little about her existence, about what humans did and how they loved. But he'd teach her, she knew. And she'd love every lesson.

She closed her eyes and listened to Uri's panting breaths. He moved faster in her, a little harder, but retained his gentleness. A delicious friction built between them, and her hips rose to meet his of their own accord, trying to match his timing. Grasping his hips, she hooked one leg around his thighs and drove him deeper. More. Needed more.

Finally, he took the hint. The sweet, tender motions grew rougher as he claimed her, mind, body, and soul. Though his muscles bunched and his fingers gripped the blankets beneath him in his attempt to hold back, she loved that he let go, her name on his lips, and she watched him, mesmerized, as he found his own release. His body went still, every muscle tense, from his biceps to his thighs. She ran her hands up and down his back, committing to memory every rise and dip of his scars, and swore she'd repay Evirax for each and every one. When he relaxed, he rested his head on her breasts, still panting. "I love you, Shadi. So damned much."

"I love you, too, Uri." More than she could say.

Chapter Eighteen

The comm's incessant beeping tore Uri from the first real sleep he'd had in ages. Unable to bear the noise anymore, he untangled himself from Shadi, who groaned but didn't wake. He pulled on his pants and swore to kill Vani when he landed on Dalara again.

"What." The only statement of greeting he'd provide at this point. Once he realized the face on the screen did not belong to his gurita friend, he swallowed roughly.

Ambassador Anita Stormbringer scowled at him. "Not the best way to greet your employer, Komandan Jacobs."

"Forgive me, ma'am. I'd expected someone else."

"I certainly hope so." Ambassador Stormbringer had been the one to give him his title, which meant he reported to her on a regular basis. "You've missed your last two appointments. It took contacting your friend on Dalara to find you." The warmth he'd come to expect from her returned to her expression. "What's happened?"

"It's a long story, Anita." But since he had time, he filled her in, not bothering to leave out Ezra's murder. "I shot Judah Welles, but I don't know if he's dead or not. Protecting Shadi was my primary goal."

"No wonder you haven't been in contact." She closed her eyes and took a deep breath. "Back on Earth, my people had a saying. 'In death, I am born.' That holds true for you more than any other man I've known."

Uri somehow managed not to roll his eyes. Anita loved her Hopi proverbs. "I don't need your sayings. I need your help."

"With finding the girl's brother? I don't know how to help you. The colony *vodja* aren't exactly sending me the names and species of their slaves."

"There has to be something...." Surely he hadn't endured all this to fail. "I promised her."

"Perhaps I can file a sanction on behalf of the human slaves, at least obtain their locations. But the system in which the nyx operate is beyond Embassy reach, Uriah. My authority is meaningless."

"It'll help. Gaining the locations of the slaves will help. We can scout each one; try to figure out where he'd be. Please, Anita. Just this one thing, and then I'll get back to—"

"Fine." Anita shook her head and pushed back a wayward stand of white hair. "But once you find the boy, you need to bring them to the Embassy. Why haven't you brought the girl already?"

Bring Shadi to a place full of strangers, let her be overwhelmed? Fabulous plan. "I did what I thought best."

"From what you told me, you probably need to stop."

Uri worked the inside of his jaw to keep his patience. "I will bring Shadi to the Embassy after we locate her brother. Which you can help us do. There are at least two humans, probably more, suffering in nyx labor camps. You didn't see me when I first escaped. Without Vani, I would have died. Is that what you want for them?"

"Of course not."

"So do what you must. Help me find Shilah, and then we'll figure out how to rescue the others."

Without another word, Anita broke the comm link.

***

As days passed without any other news concerning the human foreman on Tarbos, Shadi's obsession grew. Ever since Uri told her about his conversation with the Ambassador, she'd barely slept, afraid to sleep or leave the ship, in case Stormbringer had news. But the fact that Vani hadn't contacted them worried her. "Are you sure we shouldn't go back to Dalara?" she asked for what had to be the thousandth time.

"No. God only knows what else Evirax has sent after us."

"He might be dead."

"I know." No real emotion. As though he'd already resigned himself to the possibility.

"He's your *friend*, Uri. You have to be worried."

"Of course I'm worried." Ah, a flair of anger. "Vani helped me when I had no one. Without him...." He stopped, composed himself. "The work he does involves a great deal of risk, and he's always prepared for the inevitable. That's how he operates and how he's stayed out of trouble for so long." Taking a deep breath, he laced his fingers with hers and pulled her close. "I made promises to you, not him. He knows what he's doing. If, after we locate your brother, he still hasn't contacted us, we'll go to Dalara. But Shilah is my primary concern, because you are my primary concern." He kissed the top of her head. "How are you feeling, by the way?"

"Okay. Not too sore, if that's what you're asking."

"Good."

"Ready for more." To emphasize, she rubbed her hips against him, delighted by the resulting half moan, half growl. As far as she was concerned, she'd had plenty of time to recover, and it seemed they had enough to kill.

He hadn't been able to stop thinking about their union; every time he did, his cock twitched and his balls ached. Working for the Embassy hadn't allowed him much contact with other people, no matter the species, and she'd been so wondrously perfect. So tight, hot...so beautiful.

She wore the gown he'd picked out for her. Before that, it'd been soft pajama pants and loose T-shirts. After, he'd been so petrified he'd hurt her, but her reassurances put him at ease, and the fact that she wanted him again made him the luckiest man in the galaxy. Officially. He'd order the medal as soon as they returned to the Embassy.

Ah, damn. Stormbringer could call at any time. "We'll have to be quick."

"Fine with me. I need you inside me again. Don't care about the rest."

With a chuckle, he sat in the copilot's chair and pulled her into his lap, where she had just enough room to straddle him. "I am both hurt and flattered."

Her breathy laugh shot through him. At first sight, he had no idea she'd be able to seduce him, but God above, she did, and she didn't even have to try. "Don't be hurt. Definitely be flattered."

"Once all this is over, I'll make love to you good and proper."

"Which means what exactly?"

"Candles. A bed. Maybe soft music in the background. Me becoming acquainted with your body, learning what you like and what you love."

"I like you in me. I love you. Done." She unzipped his fly and freed his erection, grinning like she knew something he didn't. "No need to complicate things."

Should've figured she'd be the no-frills type. "Indulge me?"

"I thought I was."

When she pressed her lips to his, he groaned. Her grip on his cock tightened, and she started to stroke him. *A quick study,* he thought, wrapping his hand around hers and dictating the pace. This wouldn't be enough, but damn, it felt good. Better than good. Soon enough, he removed her hand and lifted the gown to her waist. "Same rules. If you need me to stop, tell me."

She rolled her eyes. "You'll stop saying that eventually, won't you?"

"Maybe. You're damn sexy when you're annoyed."

"I don't know what 'sexy' means, but I'm guessing it's good."

When he entered her, she moaned and pressed her forehead against his. He'd never tire of that sound of total satisfaction. Never tire of her beautiful body, so pliant and soft. "Okay?"

"Very."

He moved her hips, setting the rhythm, finding it so easy to get lost in her. Kissing her, caressing her, loving her. It'd be a miracle if he took her to the Embassy, and hell if he had to walk out of there without her.

The thought forced him to pull her closer, weave his fingers through her long hair. If she sensed his fear, she only showed it in riding him harder and wrapping her arms tight around his neck.

"Love you," she whispered, her breaths coming in short gasps. "Love you so much."

"Love you, too." Claiming her lips, he hoped to show her exactly how much she meant to him.

The comm broke Uri's concentration, but they'd reached the point of no return. Shadi's body shuddered around him; he refused to cut her pleasure short, even though every fiber of his being knew this call was about Shilah. A few more seconds passed with Shadi arching her back and crying out. As his release followed, he kissed her chest through the fabric of her gown. God, how he loved seeing her so disheveled and so satisfied.

"Should probably answer that," Shadi murmured against his ear.

"Probably, yes." Begrudgingly, he lifted her off his lap and pressed the button when she was out of sight. Anita's annoyed face filled the screen. "I hope there's news."

"There is."

Next to him, Shadi stiffened, mouth in a hard line, wide eyes imploring him to continue the conversation.

"What have you found?"

After a needlessly complicated explanation of the sanction she'd filed, she said, "I have a list of humans in nyx camps. There are...several more than I had anticipated."

Of course. Judah Welles knew the value of humans to the nyx. "Do you know where?"

"I do. I'll forward the list to you. But there's something I need to tell you."

What now? "Go on, Anita."

"Judah was confirmed dead."

"So the Welles' ring has no leader." Glancing sidelong at Shadi, he smiled.

"That isn't true."

As he remembered what Judah had said, a pang hit him in the chest and nearly stole his breath. "William."

"I'm sorry, Uri."

He nodded and turned off the comm. Time to end this. For good.

Chapter Nineteen

Uri barely moved from the pilot's chair. Shadi watched him with mild fascination and greater concern. Since Stormbringer's announcement, he'd remained stationary, hardly speaking, fingertips sometimes brushing against the hilt of his dagger. Sheer determination blazed in his eyes, and if she were honest, it scared her. This had to be the man who'd escaped the nyx. Evirax's handiwork.

She'd never wished the nyx dead more.

But she understood he had to take care of this before they found Shilah. With the Welles' group still in operation, they'd risk freeing her brother only for them all to end up re-enslaved. Besides, they didn't know which colony he worked on. They knew exactly where William Jacobs hid.

After leaving Chanterelle, the Welles' group had tucked tail and headed into deeper space, hiding on the other side of a small asteroid belt and burrowing within the rings of Irdessa, a frozen rock of a planet no one claimed. It was the closest to neutral ground they'd get.

They stopped at a fuel station to restock, and Uri bought extra guns and ammunition. He'd already forbidden her to leave the ship once they landed, but surely he knew that she went where he went. The incident with Catgut taught her not to let him out of her sight.

"You need to learn to shoot," he said, again. She vaguely remembered him asking if she knew how, but nothing ever came of it.

"Not like I can practice here."

He nodded. "When we land. You'll practice when

we land."

And become a target.

"You don't need to shoot to kill, but you'll have to be able to protect yourself in case someone comes onto the ship."

"Okay." But she would if she had the chance. The blinders had come off, and she understood what her life had been on the slaver ship—a paycheck, nothing less and, unfortunately, nothing more. She wouldn't shed a single tear over those men, least of all Uri's brother.

Of course, she planned on accompanying him, so she figured she needed to learn to kill.

During the couple of days it took to reach the asteroid belt, Shadi familiarized herself with the weapons. Learned the weight of them, the proper way to hold them, what to do if one misfired or jammed. Alone, she took apart the handgun and figured out how it worked; all the while trying to choke down the dread lingering in her system since Uri had made his decision. He hadn't been the same. His focus lay on revenge.

Truthfully, that scared her more than anything else. The sweet, loving, doting man from a few days ago had left entirely, replaced by one who barely talked about anything besides protection, had to be prodded to eat, and spent disconcerting amounts of time lost in thought. He'd had a few more conversations with Ambassador Stormbringer, but none of them changed his mind. William Jacobs had to die.

Finally, the asteroid belt came into view. Uri eased the thrusters back and surveyed the obstacle. He'd flown through these before, but this one looked far more chaotic than others he'd encountered. Some sort of flux in the gravity maybe, which made the movements unpredictable. Next to him, Shadi studied the belt, eyes narrowed and lips pursed. Then, after a few minutes, she said, "There."

He followed her line of sight and spotted the opening that would set him on a course he couldn't veer from. All the years he'd thought about killing his brother, getting the opportunity hadn't crossed his mind. It'd been a dream, a fantasy to keep him going. A fantasy about to become reality.

He opened *Gemini* full throttle and raced toward the opening. Irdessa's gravitational pull made this run tricky enough without missing the one chance he was likely to find.

Gritting his teeth, Uri narrowed his eyes and focused on the challenge. A quick dodge to avoid debris. Roll to the left to miss an asteroid. Dust and small chunks of rock pinged against the windscreen. In the copilot's chair, Shadi stared straight ahead, not even blinking, preternaturally still.

Quick turn to the right, pull back the thrusters before plowing into the next asteroid. Every time he thought they were getting close to the end, another row of rocks popped up. Weaving between them, finding the breaks, narrowly missing certain death.... It electrified him. His blood rushed in his ears, and adrenaline flowed through his body, leaving him exhilarated. It'd been a long time since he'd flown like this.

When they came through the other side, he was almost disappointed, until he remembered his mission. What he'd spent years waiting for. With his radar, he found an isolated place to land. Nestled between an ice shelf and a ridge, they were far enough away from the slaver ship to avoid detection, but close enough to avoid freezing to death before he reached it. Shadi would be secure, and it'd be safe enough to teach her how to use the weapons he'd provided.

They dressed and headed outside. The thermo gear he'd purchased blocked most of the cold and nearly swallowed Shadi whole. For the first time since Stormbringer broke the news about his brother, he smiled. "You look like a polar bear."

Though he couldn't see her face thanks to the goggles and hood, he imagined her scowl. "What is a polar bear?" By her tone of voice, she was definitely scowling.

"It's an Earth animal. A dangerous creature."

"Lethal?"

"In most cases."

"Then I'm okay with the comparison." She trudged through the snow, gloved hands clutching the rifle. Out of the array of weaponry, for some reason she'd liked that one most. "So what are we doing?"

Behind her, he lugged the other guns and the non-deadly ammo he'd gotten just for target practice. "We are going to test your aim and your acuity with your new friend there."

She patted the barrel. "Can I keep it after this is over?"

"Anything you want, love." And he meant it. For following him into this frozen wasteland without complaint, he'd give her the entire universe without her having to ask.

"Good. I want to try this out on a nyx."

"Become proficient with it, and Evirax is all yours."

Whirling around, she clutched the rifle with all the excitement of a child receiving her first toy. "Really?"

"Yes." No way could he deny her.

"You know all the ways to make me happy."

Violence and mayhem. *Simple girl with simple*

needs.

They set up about three hundred yards from the ship, where a break in the shelf provided a place to position the targets. He explained the process, showed her how to aim, and stepped away. "The kickback will be harder with this gun, just so you're aware."

She nodded. Then she shot.

The closest target shattered.

To ensure it wasn't beginners' luck, he replaced the target. Under her careful aim, it shattered, too. "How are you doing that?"

"I took the gun apart to see how it worked." She shrugged. "And I'm used to having to be precise. You have to be when it comes to threading wire."

"Show-off."

"Jealous." Her posture stiffened. "You sure you don't want me to come, too? I can help."

"Absolutely not. I'd be too worried about you getting injured. Besides," he said, wrapping his arm around her waist, "someone has to guard the ship."

"Hmph." She pulled out of his embrace. "You better come back."

"I will. Promise."

Chapter Twenty

Nights on Irdessa lasted for nearly four Earth days. Uri had waited for the cover of darkness to head toward the ship, leaving Shadi counting down the minutes until she'd slip away and follow. After all, these people had ruined her life, too, by selling it. She deserved a little bit of revenge.

Besides, she needed Uri to keep his promise. If something happened to him, she'd.... No. Better not to think about it.

Instead, she thought about the last time she'd seen her brother. By her reckoning, they'd been fifteen, and both of them had impressed Evirax with their skills. Shilah had been able to quell an argument without understanding the languages the other slaves spoke. Something about him had always been calming, and she missed his influence more than anything.

After curfew, he sat next to her and they sat in silence, looking up at the few stars able to break through Goliv's twilight. "You have to be strong," was the last thing he'd said to her.

She had to be strong for Uri. And careful. Trudging through the tundra, her feet breaking through the permafrost with every step, she moved far too slowly. Her legs burned with the exertion. Before she even got to the ship, she might pass out. *Keep going. Think about Uri. Think about Shilah. Think about shooting Evirax in the face. Head. Whatever.*

An eternity passed. Up ahead, another two hundred yards or so, she made out the silhouette of her first home. Judah had made some cosmetic upgrades, but she'd recognize the Welles' ship no matter what he did to it. Her stomach tied itself in knots, and her heart seized. For a moment, she couldn't believe she was willingly boarding, but it seemed returning to what she'd considered home for so long and laying waste to her past would be the only way to move forward in the present.

Two bodies lay across the ramp. Dead, she figured. Stepping over them, she hugged the wall and peeked around the corner. Nothing. This place had seemed so much bigger to her then, an adult's world viewed through a child's eyes. As she glanced around and found more bodies, she couldn't believe she'd ever thought it impressive. *Probably missed all the fun already.*

Curiosity led her to the cargo hold. Regardless of having seen it all of three times, she remembered the way perfectly. Sometimes, she'd joined Ezra in handing out their rations. A few shot angry looks at her, while the rest simply accepted the meager amount of food with dead, hopeless eyes. Those had always scared her most, and they still did. That they had no hope, nothing to live for.... She'd always feared becoming one of them. Uri had saved her from that.

In the bowels of the ship, she had to be more careful. On his mission, Uri would have no reason to come this way, meaning one or two of the Welles' goons might be hiding. If memory served her, there was another entrance down the corridor, and as enticing as going through the main way, shotgun blazing, sounded.... *Better to be safe.* She pressed her ear to the second door, and, sure enough, heard two distinct voices she didn't recognize. Good. That'd make the next part easier.

She eased open the door. The men stood with their backs to her, attention on the captives huddled together in the corral. No doubt they had weapons. She backed off to pump the shotgun. Though they couldn't hear it, it sounded like a bomb blast in the silent corridor.

Steeling herself, she crept into the room. No one noticed her. The guards spoke in hushed tones about what they planned to do with their cut of the profits. *They don't even know he's here.* And, no doubt, Uri hadn't thought about clearing the cargo hold. What would he do without her?

She took her time, made sure she had the proper stance, aimed, and fired. The first guard slumped to the ground, and as the second turned, she shot him in the throat. Not the head, like she'd planned, but she'd panicked. For a few seconds, she stared at the carnage on the floor, blood oozing black in the minimal light. Then she saw the prospective slaves.

Dark stains covered Uri's jacket, but every person who'd stood between him and his brother lay dead behind him. Before him, the locked door to the captain's quarters. No doubt, Judah Welles' body wasn't even cold when William took over. Pathetic.

He slipped the jacket off and let it fall to the ground. Pressing his ear to the door, he heard William's terrified voice calling for assistance that wouldn't come; he'd made sure of it.

His brother had never backed down from a challenge, though in this frantic state, he probably wouldn't open the door no matter how Uri taunted him. There might be a maintenance shaft or vent leading into the room. Or he could try to find a torch to cut the door open, but that would take too much time. He needed to get back to Shadi. So he settled for trying to lure William out. For a few minutes, he paced in front of the door, ensuring William heard his steps in the other room. Then he tried the handle again, shook it for good measure, grabbed his jacket, and stomped off to wait around the corner, dagger drawn.

As he expected, William emerged when he thought it safe. Light glinted off the gun in his hand. Of course. Knife to gun fight. Sheathing the dagger, Uri readied his pistol. No matter how much he loved the poetry of killing his brother with their family heirloom, he wasn't an idiot.

He followed William down a few corridors, taking immense satisfaction in the fact that his brother had no clue he wasn't alone. The path led to a low-tech comm room. Curious, Uri waited while William found the channel he wanted. When Anita Stormbringer's face filled the screen, Uri's heart almost stopped.

"Amnesty," William said in a voice far rougher than Uri remembered, probably aged by booze and cigarettes.

"No deal. I wanted to help you, but you pissed it away to follow Judah. I have no sympathy for you."

"Anita, *please*. I need you now. Someone is here. My men are dead."

"I don't care."

"We had a deal!" William practically screamed. "We had a deal. Your enemies enslaved for my protection."

No wonder Anita had tried to talk him out of finding William.

"The man after you is in my employ. If you can face your past, cut it down, then perhaps we can work out a deal." She cut the link.

"Bitch."

"She has that effect on a lot of people." Gun drawn, Uri emerged from the shadows.

The color drained from William's face. "Uriah. You should be dead by now."

"I'm tougher than you think."

Like a spooked animal, his brother looked everywhere for a way to escape. He was cornered, which meant Uri had to be more careful. He simply needed to pull the trigger.

"We could take her down. Take out the entire Embassy. The Jacobs brothers. What do you say?"

Take down Anita? After what he'd just heard, he had no reason to trust either of them. "It's too late for family reunions." He shot William in the left knee. With an agonized cry, his brother slumped to the ground. "I have waited years for this. Thought and planned and hoped I'd have this chance." He unsheathed the dagger. "Remember this? How easily you handed it over to Ezra Welles?"

By the man's wide eyes, he remembered.

"Remember how Mother would tell us the story of the day her grandfather received it? How important it was to her?" He shoved his brother all the way to the floor, knee to his windpipe. "You asshole, you sold our family legacy for what?"

Will tried to gurgle a response, but it didn't matter anymore. The brother he'd loved and adored died the day he gave Uri to the Welles.

Chapter Twenty-One

With a desperate shove, Will moved Uri's knee a fraction of an inch off his windpipe, just enough for him to choke out, "I've been working for the Embassy."

"So I heard." The knife's blade slipped against William's throat. "Enslaving Anita's political enemies. A shame she turned on you when you needed her most." Uri pressed harder on the steel, releasing a trickle of blood. "How does that feel?"

"It hurts," he said through gritted teeth.

"It's nothing compared to what I've lived, brother. *Nothing.*"

"I'm...sorry."

An apology? "If you think that's going to save your sorry hide, you are terribly mistaken."

"Uri, don't."

"Too fucking late."

As he started to drag the blade across his brother's throat, something hit him—*hard*—in the back of the head. Stars filled his vision, and he collapsed to the side, losing the knife in the process. Damn it. He'd forgotten all about William's gun.

While his brother tried to scramble to his feet, Uri felt around for the knife. That hit had barely missed his injury from Catgut. Nausea nearly overwhelmed him, but he had one job. One mission. He refused to fail. His fingertips brushed the hilt.

Pulling himself up, he glanced around for Will, who still tried to stand. Blood gushed from his leg, and a large amount had already pooled on the floor. At this rate, the man would bleed to death before Uri got a hit in. He approached his brother, gripping the dagger so hard his knuckles paled, and used the comm console for support. William pointed the gun at his face, but his hand shook too hard to maintain his aim. Uri ripped the gun from his brother's grasp and threw it across the floor. Then he accessed Anita's comm channel.

Sweat poured down Uri's face; his eyes failed to focus. Once Stormbringer's face filled the comm screen, he moved behind his brother and dragged the dagger across his throat. Without a word, he let William's body slump to the floor while she watched, horrified.

At least twelve pairs of eyes stared at her with awed horror. Several of the slaves were huddled together, possibly for warmth, or out of fear. She didn't recognize a few of the species, though she'd learned some were warm-blooded like humans.

Did they have translator chips? Only one way to find out. "My name is Shadi. I used to be a slave. The Welles' group sold me, but they're all dead now. You're free."

"Liar." Obscured by shadow, the owner of the voice sat in the corner of the corral. "No one comes back from the Welles."

"I did. Uri did." Maybe if she unlocked the door.... She flipped over the body of one of the guards, unfazed by the gore clinging to the headless corpse. No key. When she checked the other, she found it and opened the corral.

"How do we know you won't herd us onto another of these forsaken ships?" The questioner stepped forward, and Shadi gasped. Never had she seen a creature quite like this. Though dirty, the questioner's light-blue skin shimmered in the dim glow of the lamps. Darker-blue freckles dotted her cheeks and the arms crossed around her waist. She was nothing short of striking, with her long limbs and high cheekbones and pouty lips. But her solid-black eyes caught Shadi's attention. No pupils. No irises. And yet, they only added to the woman's beauty.

She shuddered. What sort of slavery were they intending for her?

"Are you going to answer my question?"

With a resigned sigh, she turned and lifted her hair off her neck to show the nyx's brand, the one that designated her a slave. Once she was certain everyone had had a good look, she faced the crowd. The questioner averted her eyes. "I'm sorry," she said.

"It's okay. Get out and stretch your legs. Get away from the dead. It's much warmer in the hallway, so you can warm up. I have to find Uri."

Shadi watched the slaves exit the corral, made mental notes of their conditions, which ranged from freshly beaten and starved to severely emaciated. Her heart ached for all of them, but in the back sat one who wouldn't move. A human child, she realized. Those bastards had taken another child.

She crouched and held out her arms. "Come on. You're safe now."

Large green eyes drowning in fear stared back at her. He clung to something hidden in the shadows.

To get him out, she'd have to go in there, something she'd done a handful of times as a child, but damned if she didn't remember every face she'd seen pass through the corral. And damned if the boy's wasn't the one she'd remember the rest of her life. Slowly, she crept toward him, trying to calm him with words and sounds. No good. Tears streamed down his cheeks, though he didn't make a noise. Then she saw why he stayed behind. "Oh.... Oh, sweetie."

A pale arm was wrapped around the boy, the protective clutch of a mother. Shadi's eyes stung.

Only the freezing temperature kept the corpse from smelling.

She stripped off her coat and nearly lost her breath to the frigid air, but he needed it more. Needed comfort and warmth. "Here, I know you're cold."

The fear in his eyes intensified. Leaving his mother scared him more than freezing to death, which may have been how she'd died in the first place.

"We can't stay here anymore. It's too cold." She glanced at the corpse, and then back at the boy. "Your mommy sent me to take care of you. She wants you to be safe."

He looked at his mother, like he wanted her to validate Shadi's statement. After a few seconds, he nodded.

Shadi grabbed him and wrapped him in her coat. The poor thing probably hadn't eaten in days. All bones and sunken cheeks and fear.

The other slaves had gathered in the corridor. As Shadi exited, the questioner gasped. "You got Josiah?"

"I couldn't leave him in there."

The boy, Josiah, reached for the blue-skinned alien, who took him and held him tight. "We lost Madeline a few days back. He refused to leave her side. None of us could convince him, not even the guards, so they just left her there." She lovingly stroked the boy's filthy hair back from his face. "He hasn't said a word. Not one."

"We'll get him to the Embassy. They can help."

"Okay." As Shadi turned to go, the woman said, "My name is Ath'eri, by the way."

A pleasure," Shadi replied. And it actually was.

105

Chapter Twenty-Two

She followed the trail of bodies until they ran out at a bedroom then headed down another corridor. The scent of blood, so thick she almost tasted it, tinged the air and turned her stomach. Death, she knew. She'd witnessed many a slave being put down. But blood? Blood she didn't know. Not like this.

"Uri?" she called. No response. At the end of the corridor, she spotted a closed door, and seeping from beneath it, a small river of blood. *Oh no.* Heart racing into her throat, she sprinted to the door and forced it open. Uri was slumped against a console, bloodied dagger by his side. A couple of feet away lay another body. Liam. William.

She knelt by Uri's side. When she brushed his cheek with her fingertips, he groaned and his eyes fluttered open. "Where's your coat?"

"Don't worry about that now. Are you all right?"

"Couldn't be better."

She rose and looked at his brother's body, the blown-out knee and slit throat. Eyes the same color as Uri's stared into the ceiling, forever frozen with fear. *So much fear in this place.* "We have a problem."

"Do tell."

"They took another child," she said. Rage caused her voice to tremble and her body to shake. "Took his mother, too, but she's dead. We need to go to the Embassy—"

"We can't."

"Why not?"

"Because Anita has been working with the Welles." He started to struggle to his feet. As he stumbled, Shadi caught him and steadied him, but everything for her tilted sideways. Stormbringer working with the Welles?

"How is that possible?"

"Favors for favors, love." The disgust in his voice chilled her. "We can't help the boy."

"We *have* to. Uri, he's completely alone." No way would she abandon Josiah, not when he had nowhere to go and no one to care for him. "He comes with us."

"It's too dangerous. Anita knows William's dead."

"Then we should go anyway. She's not the only human ambassador. And even so, there are plenty of other aliens waiting outside. Plenty of ambassadors to seek help from."

"God only knows who else was working with the Welles." Uri shook his head and winced. "We need to get off this forsaken planet."

"Our ship isn't big enough to hold everyone. We need a plan."

He hated it, but she was right. They did, and she wouldn't let it go until he figured out a way to help the captives. The boy. "If we go to the Embassy, we're in danger of...a great many things, the least of which is imprisonment. We need to find a place to take the captives. Some sort of halfway station."

"Better than nothing."

But they had to get them there. "Think you can pilot this junk heap?"

"Not like I have a choice. Can you make it back to *Gemini*?"

He grinned and kissed the top of her head. "Not like I have a choice."

Shadi led him down the corridors heading back toward the airlock. The group of captives stood huddled together, and he immediately spotted the boy, Josiah, wrapped in Shadi's coat. Gaunt cheeks, sunken eyes, stringy brown hair, and terrified. Then he realized who held the boy. "My lady, Ath'eri?"

The vodni'du dipped her head once and repositioned Josiah on her hip. "Komandan Jacobs, a surprise to see you here."

Not as surprised as he, but given the deal between the Welles and Stormbringer, not a total shock. "I've a feeling you somehow pissed off a certain ambassador."

"I've angered a number of people," she replied. "The least of which was Ambassador Stormbringer."

"How do you know each other?" Shadi asked.

"This is Ambassador Ath'eri of Nereus. She seconded Anita's nomination to make me a Komandan."

"He was able to locate an artifact from our home planet that brought a great deal of peace to my people." Ath'eri smiled. "It appears I'm in your debt again."

"I may need your help. First, we need to get somewhere safe." And he needed to get back to *Gemini*. Somehow. "There's a halfway station close by to get food and clean clothing."

Next to him, Shadi stiffened. "How are you going to get past the asteroid belt?"

That hadn't even occurred to him.

"We could leave *Gemini* here," she said.

"No. We'll need to ditch this ship as soon as we dock." Balls. How the hell would he make it out alive?

A ship as large as the slaver ship had to have something to help it get through an asteroid belt. It lacked the speed and maneuverability of a smaller vessel, but from what she'd seen, it didn't look damaged. "I'm going to check the main console. This ship didn't make it through that belt without some serious help." She kissed Uri on the cheek. "I'll be back."

Memory led her to the main console. One of the few times Judah had ever let her in the cockpit, he'd shown her how it all worked and let her pilot for a little while. What kind of life had he truly intended for her? What kind of life would she have?

And without Stormbringer's help, how would they find Shilah?

This entire venture had grown more complicated than she imagined possible. She slumped into the pilot's chair. In her mind, she saw Ezra standing to the side while Judah taught her the console functions. No matter how many other ships she repaired or flew, she'd always remember how this one worked.

Studying the board, she reacquainted herself with the different buttons and levers. The buttons on the far left regulated the ship's energy output, while the lever next to it opened and closed the thrusters. Judah hadn't upgraded to a touch-console, which required rewiring the entire ship, and missing that kind of time meant missing opportunities to capture people. The thought made her stomach turn.

In the middle of the console, she noticed a new button, possibly the way they'd gotten past the asteroid belt. No way to test it out here. It'd have to be a leap of faith. Either it'd work, or they'd all die.

She returned to Uri and the others. Josiah still clung to Ath'eri, his head buried in the crook of her neck. Tendrils of her hair obscured his face, but his green eyes followed Shadi's every movement. "Found a new button on the console. I'm guessing it's how they made it past the belt."

Pushing himself away from the wall, Uri nodded and wrapped his arms around her waist. "All right. I'll send you the coordinates for the halfway station.

No matter what happens, you get them there safely."

"I will." She pulled him close. "You'll meet us, right?"

"Of course."

"Promise?"

He kissed the top of her head. Then he pulled on his coat and headed out the airlock.

Chapter Twenty-Three

With the help of a maziner called Rasu, Shadi cleared the ship of the dead slavers. The enormous alien cleared most of them on his own, but she wanted to take special care of William. After she stripped everything of value from him, she and Rasu carried him far from the ship and deposited his body in a nearby ravine. Let him have the same treatment as so many of the slaves he'd sold. Once satisfied, she returned to the ship.

Time to figure out how to fly this thing.

"You know what you're doing?"

An alien like the one who had attacked her on the fuel station stood with his arms crossed over his chest, watching her study the console controls. On one side of his head, a broken horn jutted out while, on the other, just a stump. What'd happened to him?

"I think so. I've repaired some similar ships with these old consoles." Of course, repairing ships didn't mean being able to fly them. "Unless you happen to be a pilot."

The alien laughed. "That'd be convenient, huh?"

"It'd certainly help."

"Sorry to disappoint." He took a seat in Ezra's chair. "Kraale Coni, by the way."

"Nice to meet you."

"Figured we should be on good terms before we die."

Horrified, she gaped at him, but he winked and laughed again. "Sorry. It's an eibronian thing, I guess."

"Joking about death?"

"We don't take it very seriously." Kraale paused.

111

"Life is more important. You can't do anything when you're dead. Can't be anything. Can't help anyone."

Wise, for sure. "And what did you do with your life?"

"Everything I could, Shadi. Every single damn thing I could."

The same thing she intended to do after they found Shilah. "How did you get captured?"

"Trying to save a friend."

He didn't continue, and she didn't press. Instead, she focused on getting off-world and through the asteroid belt. Somehow, having Kraale with her eased her nerves. She fired up the engines and eased the thrusters open. The ship lurched upward, wobbling from side to side for a few moments before stabilizing. So far, so good.

But no word from Uri. No coordinates. Had he made it back?

Then it struck her. He hadn't promised.

No, no no no. He's okay. He's fine. Maybe the communications system isn't working. Maybe I should land and try to fix it. Figure it out. Find him. "We have to land again. I have to make sure Uri's okay."

"We have to go." Ath'eri's voice trembled. Her eyes watered with unshed tears. "Josiah is too ill to wait."

"How bad off is he?" Kraale asked.

"By Nysa's estimate, he has hours."

Hours. For a little boy. Shadi turned back to the console and wiped the tears from her cheeks. "Then we better get moving."

"I'll try to contact Josiah's father. He might be able to help us."

"Use the dark channels. I don't want Stormbringer to know what we're doing." Once Ath'eri left, she asked, "There'll be a doctor at this station, right?"

"Yeah. So long as we get the boy there quick."

She nodded and pushed the ship to its capacity. Irdessa's gravity wasn't the issue; the ship's capability was. Part of her wondered if William had risked landing on the planet in the hope that Stormbringer would rescue him. The other part said it didn't matter. Once they broke out of the planet's orbit, they had the asteroids to contend with. If she wanted a chance to see Uri again, she had to get through this damn belt.

Time to see what the mystery button did.

The moment she pushed it, a blue glow surrounded the ship, repelling the surrounding debris. She and Kraale looked at each other for a moment, and then the eibronian smiled, revealing a mouthful of sharp teeth. "We might actually make it through this."

Easing back on the throttle, she approached the obstacle at a crawl, ready to reverse the thrusters if her theory proved incorrect. But as they got closer to the belt, the asteroids that should have been pelting the ship...didn't. In front of them, a hole opened up, and in a few minutes, they were on the other side. Safe.

"Nice little button there," the eibronian said. "Explains a lot."

"Like what?"

"How they got me. How they found Nysa."

Maybe after all this ended, they could sit down and he could tell her these stories he hinted at. First, they needed to find that station. "Any idea where we're going?"

"Nope. But we don't have an opportunity to float around and hope we land on it."

Exactly what she feared. "You guys really care about Josiah, don't you?"

"When you're stuck with people, they tend to grow on you." Kraale shrugged. "Besides, his mother was a good woman. An ambassador from your people, but she had a lot of ideas to help lesser species, too."

Lesser species? "What does that mean?"

"You humans are at the top of the galactic food chain, which is why people are willing to pay so much for a human slave."

More information than she wanted. She really was only money to Ezra.

And still no word from Uri. Searching for his comm frequency, she couldn't stop the thoughts tumbling around her head—he'd died before he got to *Gemini*, or he'd gotten to the ship and something had gone wrong, or any number of things that ended with him dying all alone. Once she found it, she called his name, desperately trying to keep her tears at bay. No answer. No indication he'd reached the ship at all. She imagined the button blinking on the console with no one to push it.

But she couldn't go back. They had to do this on their own. Time for some acting.

"Is there some kind of galactic information channel?"

"Yeah. Here." Kraale leaned forward and found the appropriate channel.

"Thank you." She cleared her throat. "This is Leida Welles-Hall. I'm in need of assistance."

Someone immediately responded. "What is your situation, Mrs. Welles-Hall?"

"My father and brother are dead. I've commandeered their ship and have found multiple captives in need of medical care. If I send you my coordinates, can you direct me to the closest halfway station?"

For a moment, the comm was silent. Learning

that the two biggest slavers in the galaxy were dead had to be a shock to the system. "O-of course."

A few seconds later, she had coordinates.

"Leida Welles-Hall?" Arms crossed over his barrel-like chest, Kraale eyed her with confusion and suspicion.

"The ID I picked up after I escaped. She's out there, somewhere, but no one knows where."

"Far as I'm concerned, she can stay there." Then he said a string of words her translator chip didn't pick up, but she was fairly certain she knew the meaning.

***

After giving Kraale the controls, and strict instructions not to play with the shield button for fun, she found Ath'eri in one of the bedrooms. Still wrapped in her coat and covered in other blankets, probably as many as they could find, Josiah rested. Next to his bed stood Ath'eri and an alien with skin darker than night and almond-shaped eyes with colorless irises whose head nearly brushed the ceiling. Her hair, a violet and green mix, was a tangled and matted mess down to her mid-back. Lavender-colored raised markings decorated her arms and chest, poking through tattered remnants of a brown leather jacket. Script, maybe? Whatever it was, it looked painful.

And despite the sadness in her eyes as she watched Josiah's shallow breaths, she looked dangerous.

"Good news. We're about two hours away from the halfway station."

"If the boy lasts two hours," Nysa said, "I will be surprised."

"He lost consciousness not long after Komandan

115

Jacobs left," Ath'eri said. "All we can do is hope and try to keep him warm."

"How old is he?"

"Eight, we think. His mother didn't really talk to us much in the beginning. Well," Nysa said with a shrug, "she talked to Ath'eri, since they've known each other for a while. Madeline's husband was an ambassador."

Stormbringer had sold a human ambassador and her son to the Welles. How much lower was she willing to go?

"She'd rejected Stormbringer's proposal to recolonize Earth. Said there were too many risks involved and too much radiation to sustain any kind of life." Ath'eri brushed the hair out of Josiah's eyes. "Anita doesn't have any concept of what matters. Obviously."

"Selling a mother and son is despicable."

"Agreed," Shadi whispered. Much like selling a brother and sister only for them to be separated. "The woman is evil."

"She is," Nysa said. "It's damn time someone does something about her."

Chapter Twenty-Four

Shadi could not know about this, meaning Uri had to deal with the Embassy on his own. Selling ambassadors to slavers? What the hell was Anita thinking?

He remembered something about her wanting to recolonize Earth, a suicidal mission if ever he'd heard one. The planet's depleted ozone layer made sure nothing had a chance to survive. Even if Embassy scientists managed to repair it, colonization wouldn't happen in her lifetime. Or his.

She wanted something. Something she hadn't yet found. Something he hadn't yet found for her.

Desperate, he tried Vani's comm again. Still no reply. Then he found the slaver ship's frequency. Nothing but static.

Panic welled up in him. His hands shook, and his mouth went dry. No way to contact Shadi. No way for her to contact him. Patrols in Embassy space would ask for his identity, and he wouldn't be able to tell them. Damn it, they'd shoot him down without batting an eye, might still do it if Stormbringer had given them a directive. The idea she might have him killed drained the satisfaction of his vengeance.

He'd have to rely on stealth.

First, he had to pass the asteroid belt. Easier said than done without Shadi's sharp eyes. Easing back the thrusters, he watched and waited for his opportunity. *Gemini* could take a few hits, but not too many.

There you are. Another break in the asteroids, just large enough for the ship to squeeze through. Taking a deep breath, he opened the throttle wide and pushed the thrusters to capacity.

The first hit didn't faze him. He tried to dodge and roll, but the second hit knocked the shields down to seventy-one percent. A high-pitched warning signal reverberated in his ears, breaking his concentration. By the third and fourth hits, he barely focused. Damn it, he would *not* die here. Not until Anita Stormbringer had been brought to justice and Shadi had been reunited with her brother. He kept his promises.

More alarms sounded and the shield percentage dropped to forty-three percent. Bile churned in Uri's stomach, but he pressed forward. A little farther....

Forgive me, love.

As a large asteroid crashed into the windscreen, his world went black.

***

Shadi regretted ever doubting Vani's wisdom. Throwing Leida Welles' name around gained her more than she could've imagined. Instead of being treated as some urchin, Josiah was given the best care possible, and the others were treated with similar care and compassion. Before landing, they'd decided it best not to tell anyone about Ath'eri's or Josiah's true identities. If Stormbringer knew where they were.... She preferred not to think of that.

"Any word from Josiah's father?" she asked.

"None," Ath'eri replied. "I'm beginning to wonder if Anita has done something to him as well. Richard has always been reliable."

So he truly was all alone. "What will happen to him now?"

"I don't know." The ambassador shook her head, her tendrils of black hair shaking with the movement. "I have tried everything I can think of. Having to use the dark channels has increased the difficulty, but I can't remember him having any other family."

"Were you and his mother close?"

"No. We became sisters in captivity. I promised I'd watch out for him, but in all honesty, I won't be able to do much for him. He may go to a foster home."

That didn't sound good. "No other options?"

"Not at present. While Anita is part of the council, or alive in general, Josiah is in danger of being sold to another slaver."

"No," Shadi said. "That won't happen to him. If I have to go to the Embassy myself, I will keep him from being re-sold."

"You were young, weren't you?"

She nodded. "A little younger than him when I went into the nyx's forge for the first time. My first memories are of the slaver ship. It was my home. Ezra Welles was the closest thing I had to a father."

"Wow."

For a few minutes, they were silent. Shadi glanced around at the white hospital walls and the different pieces of art decorating them, at her coffee cup, at the floor. No word from Uri, still. Fear gnawed at her insides. He had to be okay. Had to.

***

When he was young, he'd often dreamed of returning to Earth. Of all the things he missed, he missed grass the most. The softness of it beneath his feet, the way it smelled, the vibrancy of it. The station didn't have grass. A scant few trees for oxygenation, but no grass. Just some kind of rough turf that scraped worse than the concrete.

As he came to, Uri remembered Denbury, the small English town he'd grown up in. Rolling hills covered in the softest grass and warm nights spent outside. The stories his mother would tell of their history. His favorites had always been about his great-grandfather's Zulu tribe. Brave warriors.

He had to be brave. Strong. Smart. Taking stock of the damage, he cringed. Shields at seven percent. Outer layer of the windscreen cracked. No doubt there was plenty of damage he hadn't yet seen. As long as the cloaking mechanism still worked, he'd have a chance of reaching the Embassy.

Walking out of it would be a different story.

In all his years, he hadn't yet broken a promise he'd made. If he didn't survive this, his first broken promises would be to the woman he loved.

Which meant he had to survive and escape. Eh, he'd done it before, though the Embassy presented its own dangers. He set his course and left the ship on autopilot. Time to rest and prepare for the hardest battle of his life.

Chapter Twenty-Five

Two days passed without word from Uri. Two days during which Shadi had barely slept or eaten. She, Nysa, and Ath'eri took turns keeping vigil by Josiah's bedside, hoping the boy would wake up. His vitals remained stable, but no one knew if or when he'd regain consciousness. The doctors claimed he might be trying to process the tragedies of being sold and then watching his mother die. Code for, "We don't have a clue what's wrong with him, but don't want to admit it."

During the ambassador's turn, Shadi wandered to the cafeteria. The others had long since dispersed, trying to find ways home or safe places to go, except Kraale. For whatever reason, he'd stayed, and he had no interest in explaining why, but the glances he gave Nysa told Shadi all she needed to know.

After getting another coffee, arguably the only thing keeping her alive at this point, she joined Kraale at the table he'd claimed for himself. Sometimes he'd talk; sometimes they sat in companionable silence. "How's the kid?" he asked.

So much for the silence she'd hoped for. "The same."

"Think he'll come to?"

Any optimism she'd held had dissipated as hours passed with Josiah still unconscious. "It's still early. He might surprise us."

"That's as thinly veiled a no as I've ever heard."

She shrugged. "Why do you want to kill Nysa?"

Kraale stiffened and narrowed his eyes. "You're a lot smarter than I gave you credit for being."

"Not an answer."

"See these?" He pointed to the stubs jutting from his temples. "Used to be horns."

"I've seen eibronians before."

"But you don't know about our history. We've been warring with the v'iak for a hundred cycles by now."

V'iak. She stuffed the name for Nysa's people away in her mind. "Why?"

"Because they steal our people and kill them for their horns then sell the horns for any number of things. So we started fighting back. Turns out our horns were an important part of v'iak trade. Oops," he added with a nonchalant shrug.

"So that friend you went to save...."

For a moment, Kraale seemed to consider telling the story. "All you need to know is Nysa stole my horns. I'm gonna steal her life. Fair trade, I think."

"Death is a joking matter, but your horns aren't?"

"I told you before. You can't do anything if you're dead."

Like keep your promises. "I bet Ath'eri needs a break. Please don't kill Nysa while we're here."

"Since you asked so nicely, I'll consider it."

"Thanks." She nearly knocked over her chair in her haste to leave. Wiping tears from her eyes, she searched for a vacant room and, once she found it, cried for the first time since she lost Shilah.

***

A warning beeped from the console. He'd entered Embassy space.

An armada consisting of soldiers from each represented race patrolled the tiny planet, which housed the Embassy. Getting into the atmosphere alone would be a feat, but once he landed, more soldiers would be waiting for him.

If memory served correctly, he could sneak in through the loading area. With as many deliveries as the Embassy received, and as bustling as the area typically was, he'd be able to blend into the crowd of merchants and delivery people. If someone stopped and scanned him, he'd be Oliver Hall, Athens Grove diplomat, not Uriah Jacobs, Komandan-intent-on-killing-Anita Stormbringer, but he preferred not to be scanned at all. A diplomat would be arriving to speak to the human ambassadors, and his presence would not only be noticed but recorded. Besides, Anita could refuse him. No. A scan would cause more issues. He had enough to deal with already.

Which brought him back to the flotilla. The ship's cloaking mechanism, in theory, blocked both visual confirmation and heat signature. With slow, careful piloting, he'd get past the ships. In theory.

In reality? Who knew?

He cut the engine and memorized the routes of the patrols flying between him and where he needed to go. The mental calculus of piloting in closed quarters ran through his mind until he was certain he could fly through without being detected. Unlike the thrill of flying through the asteroid belt—the first time—this required a steady hand and degree of concentration he didn't know if he possessed, especially considering the headache sitting behind his eyes and the intense pain wracking his body. But he had to do it. He had to land on Eris. Had to get to the Embassy....

Slumped against the console, he jerked awake. Shit. His condition was worse than he'd thought. Still, he'd come too far. The universe needed to learn about Anita's crimes.

He'd drifted a bit off course. Easing the thrusters, he moved back into position and began the slow descent toward Eris.

Weaving through the passing patrols, he took his time. One wrong move could expose him. Sweat poured down his face, covered his palms. His heart took up residence in his throat. Vision blurred and then sharpened. He kept moving. Kept inching forward, closer and closer to his destination, to ensuring his and Shadi's safety for another day. He'd worry about the nyx after.

Almost through.... A sudden jolt rocked the ship, throwing Uri against the console. What had he done? What could he have hit? The shield gauge dropped to two percent. One more hit of any kind would kill him. And he still hadn't breached the atmosphere.

Another alarm sounded. The cloaking had failed. The patrol ships had locked onto him. Weapons ready to annihilate the threat. With no other choice, he turned on the engines, opened the throttle, and made a last-ditch effort to land while the ship screamed in his ears, high-pitched sirens warning of imminent doom, quite possibly the last sound he'd ever hear. He thought of Shadi's sweet voice, her large green eyes, and her gentleness, of the promises he'd made her. If the fates had any mercy, they'd allow him to keep the most important one.

Deep in his gut, he knew Anita had information about Shilah. Knew it like he knew his own name. With the entire Welles' group dead, she had no one to protect her, no reason to keep her secrets. No reason not to help him.

First, he had to make it to the ground.

The targeting console was fried, but Uri didn't need it. A moving target was much harder to hit, and the ship still had most of its mobility. Flying like a madman, he barrel-rolled, zipped from side to side, and changed speeds—anything to throw off his pursuers. When he passed into Eris' atmosphere, he whooped and tried to figure out his next move. At this point, he needed to land *somewhere*, preferably close to the Embassy where he could disappear into a crowd.

There. A clearing only a few yards away from the south entrance. *Excellent*.

With his speed maxed out, he had to wait. This would by far be the dumbest thing he'd ever done, but considering his dire situation, he had no choice. A shame to waste such a lovely ship....

He ran to the airlock, head pounding and heart thundering in his ears, and pressed the button to open it. The timing had to be perfect.

I love you, Shadi, he thought. Then he jumped.

Chapter Twenty-Six

The holy-shit-I'm-alive feeling only lasted a few seconds. Uri forced himself to his feet. *Gemini* lay in a crumpled heap, a mile-long rut in its wake. The stench of fuel tainted the air, and his stomach churned like he'd devoured an entire quarry. He had minutes, maybe, to get as far away from the ship as possible. He darted into the trees, moving south and west, trying to skirt around to the merchants and delivery people milling around the loading area. Once he got lost in the crowd, he'd be—

BOOM. The ship's explosion threw him to the dirt. Covering his head with his arms, he waited for the ground to stop shaking before he tried to move. Trapped. He was trapped on this blasted planet.

Desperation got him to his feet, and he dusted the dirt and leaves from his pants. Having a finite amount of time left—both to accomplish his goals and to live—spurred him toward the crowd, who had stilled at the spectacle of the fireball that used to be his ship. Their ship. He hadn't gotten to tell Shadi good-bye. Didn't know where she was, if she was safe. If the boy had lived. As he pushed it from his mind, he slipped into the throng and headed toward the entrance. Hopefully, the fire would keep the guards occupied long enough for him to search Anita's office.

No matter how many times he visited the Embassy, he never adjusted to the opulence the ambassadors apparently needed to perform their duties. Rich stones and woods from various planets decorated the grandiose halls, creating odd mosaics of galactic harmony; marble tiles led the way to the ambassadors' offices; plants representing each species—hearty prairie grass for humans, deadly singing glass for the v'iak, full-bodied blue sea roses for the vodni'du, a strange rock-like plant he could never remember the name of for the maziners—lined the walls. It all worked so hard to propagate the message of aliens working together and singing songs of peace and love when, in reality, the slaves on the Welles' ship had gotten along better than the ambassadors ever did. What was the old adage about absolute power? Obviously, Anita hadn't bothered with remembering it.

Keeping his eyes and ears open for guards, he picked a careful path toward the ambassadors' offices. Sweat poured down his face and his breaths came in shallow gasps, but he kept moving, kept thinking of Shadi and how this would help her find her brother, bring her peace. God above, he hoped she'd find peace.

Finally, he located Anita's office, denoted by the sun-like symbol of Tawa, the Hopi creator god, carved into the large cottonwood door. He shook his head. How many times had he looked at this door, at the woman behind it, and believed she had the best intentions in her heart, not just for humans, but for everyone in the galaxy? How many times had he done what she asked without question or hesitation? That anger, that betrayal, fueled him. He forced open the door, prepared for a confrontation too long in the making.

She was gone.

The adrenaline flooding his system dried up. Legs almost crumpling beneath him, Uri stumbled toward the desk and leaned against it for support. Disbelief replaced the adrenaline and weighed down his body until he felt like living lead. So tired. So fucking tired....

No time for rest. He booted up Anita's computer, bypassing the log-in screen with ease. Vani had taught him well. Breaking into her encrypted files proved a bit more difficult, but once he input the right codes, a treasure trove of incriminating information lay before him, including messages between Anita and William. Curiosity got the better of him. A few keystrokes revealed hundreds of deleted messages from William then Judah then Ezra. Without reading them, he uploaded them to the server he and Ath'eri had used when he'd searched for her people's relic, but one caught his eye. He tapped on the screen and the message opened, filling the screen with information he wished he hadn't seen. "Shit," he whispered.

The door opened. The short burst of energy had him on his feet, hand gripping the butt of his gun. In walked Ioan Gregory, acting ambassador in his missing wife's stead. "Uri?"

"Where is Anita?" he ground out.

"The Galactic Unity summit." Ioan narrowed his green eyes, eyes Uri had seen somewhere else.... "What the hell happened to you?"

"I must speak with her immediately." Unholstering his gun, he said, "You will take me to her." Ioan's eyes widened at the sight of the gun. Grabbing him by the shoulder, Uri turned the man around and pressed the barrel into his side. "Now."

***

After another day of watching Josiah sleep, Shadi needed to rest, herself. Thankfully, the hospital staff had been kind and accommodating, but she feared the boy wouldn't wake up. Ath'eri refused to admit defeat, and Shadi envied her. After all the death she'd seen under nyx servitude, she had no idea how to hope.

As with every other time she'd tried to rest, her weary body sank into the hard cot, but her mind chose to cycle through the worst possible outcomes for Josiah, for her brother, and of course, for Uri. The lack of contact pressed down on her until she walked hunched over, not really seeing or hearing anything, unable to care. She pressed on for Shilah and the ghost of her optimism. Nothing more.

Her eyes fluttered closed. Maybe, this time, sleep would claim her, calm her, and when she awoke, she'd be in Uri's arms on *Gemini*, and none of this would have ever happened. Josiah's mother would still be alive, and he'd be awake, telling his wild stories and asking strange questions of the other captives with a child's innocence.

"Shadi!"

Nysa.

Shadi scrambled up from the cot, heart hammering against her ribs. Was it Josiah? But, no...Ath'eri was with him. Then, what?

She followed Nysa to the cafeteria where diners and workers alike were transfixed by the image on the television—thanks to Kraale for providing the term. Gripping the v'iak's hand, she watched the scene unfold almost in slow motion. The sounds in the cafeteria died away. Even Nysa's hand on hers no longer registered.

Uri. The joy of his being alive was overshadowed by his actions. He stood next to a human man, gun drawn at the other ambassadors. At Anita. Though she couldn't hear what he said, she read his intentions loud and clear.

"By the ancestors," Ath'eri said. When she'd gotten there, Shadi didn't know, but she grabbed the ambassador's hand for the extra support. "What is he doing?"

"He's going to kill Stormbringer," Nysa replied. "And good riddance."

But before he fired a shot, a horde of guards surrounded him, wrenching the human free from Uri's grip and forcing Uri to his knees. Above the chaos, he shouted a word Shadi didn't know. Over and over.

The television went black.

Frozen with fear, Shadi simply breathed, attention still on the screen, as though it'd magically show her what she wanted to see. Ath'eri sprinted out of the cafeteria, and Nysa tore her hand away to wrap Shadi in her arms and hold her quaking form.

They sat at the nearest table. A strange muttering filled the room. Were they still safe here? "What just happened?"

Nysa's colorless eyes were rimmed with tears. "I think your mate just got himself killed."

Chapter Twenty-Seven

Shadi woke feeling rested and relaxed for the first time in ages. She stretched, a familiar chorus of cracks and pops filling the silence, and looked around for Uri. Then she remembered.

Still a little groggy, she pulled against the restraints cuffing her wrists to the bedrails, but they were too tight. Her throat went dry. The monitors around her broke into frenzied beeping. A hand forced her back against her pillows. "Shadi, it's Ath'eri. You're okay."

"Uri," she said. "We have to find him. We have to get him back."

"I agree."

Looking into the ambassador's lovely face, she saw only fierce determination. "You love him?"

"No. The one to whom I'd pledged my heart has long since passed." She took a deep breath, as though cleansing herself of the hurt. "As I said, I owe him a great debt. And I respect him."

"What did he keep saying?"

"*Diam'ca.* It's an old word in my language meaning 'secret.' The name of a server he and I had used to trade information when he was searching for that relic." Ath'eri leaned forward and rested her head on the bedrail. "He uploaded a great deal of information to it that could cause the Embassy to crumble."

"Good riddance," Shadi muttered.

"There's something you should see as well, which pertains to your brother."

The monitors beeped again in a strange rhythm

matching her heartbeat. "Shilah?"

The ambassador nodded. "I'll see about getting you released. Then I'll show you what Uri found."

***

A couple hours later, Shadi glared over Ath'eri's shoulder at the computer screen. Right there. In Anita's hands this entire time.

Shilah's location.

Her breath hitched in her throat, and twin emotions of relief and sorrow filled her as she clutched the edge of the desk so hard her knuckles turned white and the plastic bit into her hands. Uri had trusted this woman; as a result, so had she. Anita Stormbringer had betrayed them both.

"There's more," Ath'eri said, her voice thick with emotion.

What else? "Just tell me."

"It's about Ioan Gregory, Josiah's father." She gestured to a nearby chair. "You should sit."

Promptly, she did.

"According to correspondence between Anita and Ezra Welles, Ioan's father was unfaithful. Out of wedlock, he fathered a set of twins."

"I see where this is going, and I'm not sure I want to hear the rest."

Undaunted, Ath'eri continued. "Since Colin Gregory was a highly-respected ambassador, Anita offered to 'take care of the issue.' Which resulted in your mother being sold to the Welles' group when you and your brother were babies. According to these emails, your mother died before being purchased. So the Welles took you and Shilah as restitution. Raised you and trained you to be specialists."

Bile shot into Shadi's throat. She forced it back down.

"Once she received confirmation you'd been sold, she turned her attention back to Colin and told him that unless he did exactly what she wanted, she'd let the information leak and set him up as the one who'd had you sold."

If she'd had any bit of emotion left, she'd scream and cry and yell about how her life had been ruined for Stormbringer's blackmail material, but watching Uri's arrest had drained the last of it out of her. "Ioan Gregory is my half-brother."

"Which makes Josiah your nephew."

Shadi nodded. "And, therefore, my responsibility."

"Yes." Ath'eri narrowed her eyes. "Are you all right?"

"Believe me, after everything I've been through, surprises no longer register." She stood and headed toward the door. "Josiah will be safe here, right?"

"He will."

"Good. I'm going after Uri." *I'm sorry, brother, but he needs me. And I'll need him to find you.*

"You'll need a plan."

Point.

"And help."

Second point. "Tell Kraale and Nysa to meet me at the ship."

***

An insistent muttering drew Uri from unconsciousness. Opening his eyes...well, it was dark enough that he couldn't be sure his eyes were actually open. He lifted his hands and couldn't see them, but he felt the cuffs on his wrists, reminiscent of the fahir's. He groaned. Fabulous. Jail.

He'd heard stories of the Embassy's prison, in which were kept the lowest of the galaxy's low.

Situated on the other side of Eris and built in the heart of a dormant volcano, the prison was rumored to be inescapable, its mercenaries-turned-guards both ruthless and expendable. And, as he'd always heard, most rumors had their roots in truth.

"'Bout damn time you woke up."

He smiled at the voice that, no matter how dark the situation, always brought a bit of joy into his life. "So they got you, eh?"

"Yeah. Looks like gurita aren't prepared for *every* situation. Just 99 percent of them."

As his eyes focused, he made out Vani's outline, and the relief of knowing his best friend was alive faded with the realization of how dire their situation had become. "I'm assuming the one percent is being captured by the Embassy."

"We have a winner. Also, we have a...how do I put this...guest."

The mumbling stopped. "Talking about li'l ol' me?"

"Yep."

To Uri's right, a door opened, throwing a shaft of light into the dismal room and illuminating the woman. Though her hair was ratty and disheveled and dirt smeared her face, her resemblance to Ezra Welles couldn't be denied. She met the guard entering the cell with defiance and didn't speak a word until he'd left. "Insolent assholes, all of them."

"Sound like somebody you know?" Vani asked.

He went through his mental catalogue of familiar voices and speech patterns but came up empty in his exhaustion. "I'm not in a mood for these games, my friend."

"Too bad. You'd been doing so well." Vani paused. "That, my dear Komandan, is the love child of Ezra Welles and Anita Stormbringer."

Chapter Twenty-Eight

Anita and Ezra? It all made so much sense. Possibly too much. "William only thought *they* had an agreement," he said. "He must not have known about her involvement with Ezra."

"As far as I know, nobody did. They assumed Miss Leida here belonged to Judah's mother and that she didn't want her impressionable little baby foo-foo exposed to such horrible, awful, no-good criminals like Ezra. Anita wasn't on anybody's radar."

Uri bit back a laugh at Vani's terrible impression of a haughty human woman. Still, this was *the* Leida Welles. "She's been here for how long?"

"Six years, and you can stop talking about me like I'm not even here." The chains rattled as Leida moved around. "Like I'm just some voice in the darkness."

"Sorry," Vani said, actually sounding apologetic. "Kinda easy to forget, I guess."

"If story time is over, can we please figure out how to get out of here?"

Uri agreed. They needed a plan. "Do either of you know anything of the prison's layout?"

"Of course," Leida answered.

"No offense, princess, but you've been here for six years. How can you know anything?"

"Because the path from the ship bay to this cell is the last thing I saw before they threw me in here. I've recited it to myself every day."

That explained her mutterings.

"Straight, left, left, straight, straight, right, straight, right."

"So if we follow that backward, then we'll get to...somewhere." Safety seemed too good to be true, considering that even if they escaped, Evirax would still be out there, waiting.

"Essentially."

Good. Time to make a plan.

***

By the time Shadi reached the ship, Nysa had Kraale in a headlock, saying something about how his horns were too shitty to fetch a good price. "Knock it off, you two. You can kill each other later."

"I was winning, too," Nysa said.

"Only because I let you."

"Children. Now." Already, she wondered if choosing them had been a good idea, but she needed them both. From what little Ath'eri had told her, she needed help to breach the prison.

They settled into the large bedroom that had apparently doubled as a makeshift meeting space. Kraale and Nysa still glared at each other from across the table. "We're doing a jailbreak."

That got their attention.

"Uri is in prison. It's all over the news. According to Ath'eri, there will supposedly be a trial, but chances are that they'll wait long enough for the story to blow over, and then they'll kill him." She sighed. "I'm not going to let that happen to him. Not when he's risked his life over and over for me."

"What do you need, Shadi?" Leaning over the table, the v'iak took her hand.

"Support, more than anything. People I can trust. I'm in as much danger as Uri right now." She swallowed. "So is my brother. We have to work fast and under the assumption that everything has been compromised." *Including my super-useful ID.*

"What do we do?" Kraale asked.

"We steal a ship and head to the prison. Once there, we'll fight our way in, find him, and get back out."

"Straightforward. I like it."

Nysa snorted. "You would. Eibronians are all brawn. No brains." For emphasis, she tapped the side of her head.

Offering a smile, Shadi said, "We still need a ship."

"Nysa's the thief." Kraale crossed his arms over his large chest and glared at the v'iak like he expected her to challenge him.

To his disappointment, she shrugged. "You have to play to your strengths, right?"

"Yes."

Shadi jerked at Ath'eri's sudden entrance. Dressed in an obvious hand-me-down outfit of plain brown trousers, a too-big tunic shirt, and boots that didn't quite fit, she still cut an imposing figure.

She stepped into the room and took a seat next to Kraale. "I found us a ship."

"Us?" No way. "It's too dangerous for you. You saw how Stormbringer kept track of everyone she sold to the Welles. She'll know you weren't sold."

"I'm not going to sit and let others risk their lives. I did that for eleven cycles. Uri nearly died to retrieve a relic I should have gotten myself. I will fight my own battles."

"What about—"

Ath'eri cut Nysa off with a cold glare. The other woman squirmed in her seat.

"Who'll stay with Josiah?" Shadi asked. Since learning of their connection, the boy hadn't been far from her mind. "He doesn't have anyone except you."

"I know. But this must be done." The ambassador's voice held a finality to it that Shadi recognized. Uri's had held that same note. No words would change Ath'eri's mind.

"All right, then. Let's go see that ship."

***

The ship wasn't a class or model Shadi recognized. As she studied the console, she cast sidelong glances at Kraale, who hadn't said a word since they exited the other ship and instead ran his fingertips over the controls like a lover caressing his beloved, murmuring softly in a language her translator didn't pick up. "Need a few minutes alone?" she teased.

Smirking, he moved away and sat. "I don't know how she did it."

"How who did what?"

"How Ath'eri got this ship. *This* ship. Could've gotten any other one in the galaxy." When Shadi didn't speak, he continued in a nostalgic tone. "I haven't seen her in a long time. Built her when I was a kid. First cruiser I ever worked on."

"You built ships?"

"I did." He grinned. "For the eibronian military. I wanted to do something to help." Leaning over, he lifted his left pants leg and revealed a prosthetic that almost matched his skin tone, but not quite. "Lost my leg in a v'iak raid. After that, I swore I'd find a way to kill as many of the bastards as I could."

"Including Nysa."

"Especially Nysa. Her mother is the reason I lost my leg." He shifted and turned back to the console. "V'iak huntresses are galaxy renowned for their skill. They *never* leave empty-handed. When I escaped, the other huntresses killed her mother for failing."

All of this for revenge. She missed the days when she and Uri were running from Catgut, when things seemed simpler. "So you can fly this?"

"In my sleep."

"Good. Ath'eri is getting the coordinates." Mind reeling, Shadi left to find a quiet spot. She needed to be ready for whatever the prison had in store.

Chapter Twenty-Nine

They spent a couple of days letting Uri rest before implementing their plan. While Leida had spent her time reciting the path back to the entrance, Vani had been learning the guards' routines. Though they had no access to outside light, gurita had a highly dependable internal clock, a trait that had developed over the course of their evolution. Putting together all the information, they were able to begin planning.

One drawback to their plan—the volcano itself. Over the last several days, it'd been rumbling more than usual, according to Leida, and Uri had noticed a temperature increase. The odds of an eruption were uncomfortably high, meaning they needed to implement their plan ASAP.

"The ship bay is full of single-passenger cruisers," Vani said, drawing Uri's attention back to the conversation, "but I spotted a couple larger ones that might make for decent getaway vehicles."

"Good to know."

"But it's on the roof. There's an access lift, if we can get to it. No idea if there are stairs."

"We'll have to get weapons, too," Leida said. "They took my guns when they caught me. I want them back."

"What were you doing anyway, princess? How'd they get you?"

"And why?" Uri asked.

"I'll explain once we're safe."

Fair enough. They didn't need any distractions.

When the guard came with their evening *meal,*

they sprang into action. Being nearest the door, Leida moved in behind him and used her chains to choke him out. Using the slice of light from the still-open door, she patted him down and found the keys, quickly unlocking her shackles. Without hesitation, she moved to Vani and then to Uri.

He got to his feet and took the guard's pistol. "Any idea where they'd keep your guns?" he asked.

Leida answered with a subtle shake of her head.

Great. "We can't waste time."

Chewing the inside of her jaw, she relented. "They were Anita's anyway."

No one else patrolled the hallway—yet. Uri's pulse thumped in his ears. He mentally recited Leida's directions as a way to calm himself. No one needed to know how badly he shook.

They'd navigated two hallways before coming across another guard, whom Leida knocked out with a quick hit to the temple. She grabbed a baton and a gun from the guard's belt, as though she needed them. No doubt, she had her mother's fiery temper to complement her father's strength.

Soon enough, the lift to the docks came into view. Two guards stood watch, and there was no good way to flank them. Glancing from Leida to Vani and back to the guards, Uri tried to calculate their odds without firing. Abysmal, to say the least. He'd have to fire and risk alerting every guard in the vicinity.

He had the advantage of cover, though. The other men were out in the open. *Two quick shots....*

The first caught one guard in the neck, and the second missed entirely. "Get to the dock," he said. "Find a ship. I'll be there as soon as I can."

***

For the last several days, Shadi had listened to

the radio almost nonstop, waiting for updates concerning Uri's trial. Given how public his arrest was, it'd been the talk of galactic news and radio hosts, most of whom had decried his attempted assassination as she'd expected. No one truly knew how dangerous Anita Stormbringer could be. Or maybe they did, and this was their way of avoiding a similar fate.

Shotgun in hand, she headed to the cockpit. Without looking, Kraale motioned her forward. "See that?" he asked, pointing to a volcano. "Hasn't erupted since they built the damn prison." He gestured to a screen on the console. "*Swazo* has a mounted camera to assist with landing." After he pushed a small button, the screen came on. He didn't speak again until they were positioned over the opening. "Those orange-looking fissures are lava pushing through to the surface."

"How long do you think we have?"

"Long enough to get in, get Uri, and haul ass."

She nodded. No room for mistakes. "All right then. Let's land."

"Well, there's one other problem." Zooming in, the camera revealed what looked like a firefight on the topmost deck. "Multiple shots being fired from the south. One shooter here"— he tapped the screen near what looked like a sizeable ship—"and another figure."

Uri, maybe, but who was with him?

"I can open fire from here."

"Don't. We need to know what we're shooting at first. I don't want to risk hurting someone who doesn't deserve it."

"Shrewd but respectable."

"I do my best."

While Kraale swooped around to the west, she sought out Nysa and Ath'eri. "There's a firefight on the roof. Nysa, you, Kraale, and I are going to hop down and take cover behind the ships. Possible allies are to the north—one armed, one unarmed. Ath'eri, I need you up here, maintaining our altitude and using the turret guns if necessary to provide us some additional cover."

The women nodded their agreement.

Shaking with trepidation, Shadi shouldered her shotgun. If Kraale and Nysa couldn't work together, she, Uri, and whoever else was on the rooftop were as good as dead.

***

Two guards down, and from the sound of the dull thuds echoing through the lift tube, at least a half dozen more waited for him on the rooftop. Adding to that the increasing frequency of the tremors rattling the prison and the rise in temperature.... They needed to dispatch those guards as quickly as possible.

Another rumble shook the prison. Uri swore under his breath and charged his pistol. At least he'd have the element of surprise in his favor.

The lift doors creaked open, and the dull thuds he'd heard turned into deafening shots. In a quick tally, he counted eight guards and four bodies—that he saw. Not bad, given how long it'd been since Leida fired a gun.

However, the steam rising from the volcano obscured the surrounding area. Who knew how many other guards there were? Wiping sweat from his forehead, he moved to cover at the boxy nose of a transport ship, possibly the same one he'd been in. He pressed flush against it and waited for his opportunity. A guard stepped out to fire, and Uri picked him off with a clean headshot then stepped back into cover, shielding himself and hopefully confusing the others.

Of course, when another ship flew overhead, everyone was confused, including him. What now? Could be the nyx, could be anything.

With the guards distracted, Uri picked his way toward what he hoped to be Leida's location, taking out another guard in the process. He glimpsed his temporary ally through the steam. Sweat matted her hair to her face, and eyes the same shade of brown as Anita's squinted. She somehow shot a guard in the thigh.

A few moments later, the v'iak and the eibronian from the slaver ship joined them. Which meant....

"Volcano's gonna blow soon," the eibronian said. "Get to the ship. We'll cover you."

"Where is Shadi?" Then the shotgun blast sounded from his right. "Never mind."

He moved to the other side where he could help Shadi flank the guards while the others headed toward the ship. From his position, he heard the elevator doors open again, and he cursed under his breath. Moving into position, he nailed two of the new squadron before they had a chance to fire. He glimpsed Shadi out of the corner of his eye. Her long hair was pulled away from her face, clothes covered in dust, sweat dripping down her face and neck. The temperature was steadily rising, the vibrations beneath his feet growing even stronger, more frequent. Pockets of steam jetted through the grated floor. They needed to go—*now*.

Seemed she had the same thought. After a couple quick shots, she jerked her head back toward the ship. He nodded. Time to get the hell off this rock.

Around the pillar, lava started shooting up, some of it splattering on the ground, the other ships, and the guards. He and Shadi dodged lava like scalding raindrops while the guards scrambled to the nearest ship to try getting off the pillar in time. More geysers of lava gushed up from the volcano's throat. Those guards weren't going to make it.

Shadi's scream refocused him. She clutched her arm, the pain seeming to freeze her steps. He pressed his hand into the small of her back and mumbled to her, urged her to keep moving. No matter how bad her injury, stopping would kill them both. "Almost there, love. Almost there. Cover your mouth."

She answered him with agonized groans.

Ahead of them, the eibronian waved them forward, while the ship slowly wobbled off the ground. Shadi reached for him, and he pulled her into the transport then reached for Uri. Another pocket of steam shot up blocking Uri's path. Behind him, the footsteps of the remaining guards reverberated on the steel. He lifted his foot; the soles of his boots were beginning to melt. Unwilling to be separated from Shadi again, he pivoted and took off in a sprint toward a clearer area of the platform. He'd have to double around and try to reach the ship from another angle.

Only adrenaline and determination kept him from giving up and crumpling to the ground. His lungs burned from the steam and the exertion, but he'd come too far. She'd come too far. All that mattered was boarding that damn ship.

In the airlock, Leida and the v'iak picked off the guards while he raced toward them. Willing every last bit of strength into his legs, he leapt as the platform dipped to the side. The eibronian pulled him onto the ship just in time to watch the entire prison tumble. "Get us out of here," the eibronian called.

The ship lurched upward. As the anti-grav stabilized, the volcano erupted.

Her arm burned, but she had to get to the

cockpit. Nysa trailed behind her, yelling, but she didn't listen. Ath'eri couldn't get them out of this.

"Move," she growled. The ambassador didn't hesitate. Shadi stabilized the anti-grav and opened the throttle before pushing the thrusters to the max. If she could get out of the volcano's throat, they had a chance.

As a cloud of ash enveloped the ship, Shadi cursed and tried to remember what Judah had taught her about flying blind. She closed the throttle and eased the thrusters back. The front camera didn't help. Seconds passed like hours, and the ash cloud seemed to stretch forever. She angled up farther, hoping to find a thinner part to fly through. Surely, closer to the top....

All of a sudden, she came out the other side— only yards from the volcano wall. "Shit!" she yelled. She pulled back on the steering column and skirted the wall by mere feet. Lava spewed around them, but they'd made it. Holy shit, they'd made it.

After breaking Eris' orbit, she turned to Nysa. "Let's never do that again, okay?"

"I fully agree, *mis'cha*."

"What does that mean?"

Pressing the compress to her arm again, the huntress smiled. "I don't think there's a good human translation. The closest would be 'lucky lunatic.'"

Sounded about right.

Chapter Thirty

With their course safely plotted and Embassy space behind them, Uri took the first real breath he'd had in a while. Shadi slept curled into him, sometimes whimpering or groaning. They didn't have the necessary treatment onboard for her burn, and he feared it'd become infected before they returned to the hospital. After all, they had days of travel ahead.

Vani and Leida hadn't fared much better. Ath'eri had done what she could, but they all needed medical attention. They needed rest.

He changed Shadi's bandages every few hours, and each time, he lost hope she'd escape infection. The salve did nothing to help her heal. If they'd endured all this for him to lose her.... No. She would fight. She would see her brother again. He'd make sure of it.

"How is she?"

He started at Leida's voice. She leaned against the frame, arms crossed, showing off well-toned biceps and a few scars of her own. Her dark hair hung straight down her back, like Anita's, and her eyes were brighter. Still, she looked pale, tired. He guessed they all did. "Bad," he replied. "She's feverish. Hasn't woken up for hours now."

"Have you been using cold compresses?"

Nodding, he moved Shadi's sweat-soaked hair from her face. "Between Ath'eri and me, we've tried everything we can think of. The infection is worsening every minute."

"Ezra wasn't one to keep medical supplies on hand." She sat on the edge of the bed, face scrunched in concentration. "We can try putting her in a cool shower."

"Ath'eri suggested the same. Brought her fever down a few degrees, but it shot back up after a couple of hours."

"The big guy's an eibronian, right?"

"Yes." What was she getting at?

"I'll be back."

Almost half an hour later, Leida returned with a syringe filled with a dark-blue substance. As she prepped Shadi's arm, she spoke. "One time, when I was working in the Qanope cluster, the only other human on my team came down with a horrible infection. We didn't have the tools to treat him, but someone mentioned how eibronian blood acted as a panacea for most of the major species, which is why they haven't been permitted into the Embassy. I wasn't one to believe in fairy tales, but desperate times, you know." She injected the syringe and pushed the plunger. "I ended up going to a black-market shop on Agrila to find eibronian blood. Paid a shit ton for it. Within hours, though, Trey was back on his feet."

Uri had heard about the crisis in the Qanope cluster. Dominated mostly by maziners, planets there suffered some of the worst poverty and disease in the known universe and were often an easy target for rogues and...slave traders. "You said you'd tell us how you got caught once we were safe. I believe it's time for that story."

She nodded. "I used to work for a nonprofit that operated in some of the shittiest places the universe had to offer. I'd changed my name, since absolutely *no one* wanted to deal with the Welles or the Embassy, and neither did I. Out of necessity, we became almost a mercenary group, just to protect ourselves while we traveled to all these horrible places. Our ship always had top-of-the-line med equipment, medications, everything we'd need to treat people who needed our help. At first, we stuck to humans, but it became obvious that we needed to broaden our scope. So we did. Our designation as a non-profit gave us the leeway to do that."

A faraway look entered Leida's eyes. "But the Embassy didn't like it, because we were doing what they should've been all along. I hadn't seen Anita since I was fifteen. Everything I'd learned about medicine, I learned on the job. By the time I turned twenty-two, I was leading my own team. Unfortunately, I led them into a trap. We'd gotten a call about an outbreak of cave fever among a camp of uroks, so, of course, I responded. When we landed on Gormut, though, the Embassy was waiting for us, even though they were well out of their jurisdiction. They arrested us on bullshit charges and brought us back to Eris for 'trial.'"

"I remember that. The Komandan were outraged. Quite a few of them broke rank afterward."

"Why didn't you?"

"To avoid the forge," he said slowly.

Understanding softened Leida's face. "I'm sorry."

"It will be worth it, if she wakes up."

"Give the blood time to work. I'll thank Kraale for it on your behalf." She left.

Chapter Thirty-One

A faint beep interrupted Shadi's dream, and the image vanished, taking with it her thoughts of her brother. Forcing open her eyes, she glanced around a foreign room; pain registered at the edge of her perception, and then, suddenly, it was on her like one of the scavenger beasts on Goliv, with sharp claws and teeth like razors. The beeps raced into an alarming staccato.

"Shadi." Strong hands rested on her undamaged shoulder. She whimpered, but when Uri's face registered in her brain, she threw her arms around him. Everything came back to her—his arrest, their half-baked plan to save him from execution, the firefight on the rooftop, and the jet of steam that scalded her right arm. Pulling away, she examined the bandage covering her from shoulder to elbow. "How bad?" she asked.

"Bad enough. You suffered quite a bit of damage, love." Uri shook his head, eyes downcast. Even exhausted and beaten, he was still handsome. She reached for his hand, loved seeing his dark skin against hers. "I could've lost you," he said. "You shouldn't have—"

"I wasn't going to let them kill you. I told you I can't do this without you, and as long as I breathe, I will not be separated from you." Wearily, she lifted her left hand. The wedding ring glinted in the light. "This means something to me now. You mean everything."

"As do you." He stroked her hair and gave her the warm smile that convinced her everything would work out. She wondered if he knew about her parentage, if he'd read any of the emails he'd sent to Ath'eri or if he just copied Anita's entire database. When she looked at him, though, she didn't want to think about the lies and the tragedy of it all. Didn't want to think of what could have been. Her life and her brother's life had been dictated by people who cared nothing for them, who'd used them for personal gain. Time to dictate her own life.

"Marry me," she said.

Momentarily, his eyes went wide. "What?"

"Marry me." She struggled to sit up. "I love you. And I can't imagine my life without you."

"How can I say no to that?" Leaning over, he kissed her gently and pressed his forehead to hers. "Once all this is over—"

"No. Now. Today."

"You're serious."

"Yes." How could she put into words the paralyzing fear she'd experienced when she hadn't heard from him, the terror of seeing him arrested and thinking she'd never see him again? She didn't know much about humans, but she knew the importance of the commitment she wanted to make. "I want you forever. I have no idea what will happen after today, whether Evirax will come after us or send someone else, or whether we'll bring Stormbringer down, so I want to make it count."

"Then, yes. It'd be my honor."

***

By evening, Shadi stood in front of a mirror looking at the woman she'd become over the course of the last few months. Though no amount of time could erase her years of servitude to the nyx, she had hope for the future. This first step cemented that she'd have one, and that she'd spend it with the man she loved.

Ath'eri fussed with the finishing touches. While Shadi had waited for the doctor to clear her, her friends had been busy procuring what they'd need for their makeshift ceremony, and somehow, they'd managed to find a suitable dress, enough gauzy material for a veil, and flowers. Why a human ceremony required all of this, she didn't know, but Ath'eri coached her through the scaled-down version with her impeccable poise and grace. "This kind of ceremony is one of the oldest and simplest of human ceremonies." she said. "But, to me, it's one of the most beautiful, as well."

"You've performed human ceremonies?"

"Yes. Some human women are enthralled with our culture and choose to commit to a vodni'du. As a sign of respect, most vodni priestesses learn the human rituals."

"What about human males?"

"It's...not the same."

Shadi nodded along and tried to remember everything she was told.

"If you forget something, I'll help you. There." Behind her, Ath'eri smiled. "You look beautiful."

"Thank you."

"Maybe someday we can have a more elaborate ceremony."

"And Shilah can be there." The pang of his absence shot through her.

"Exactly."

She adjusted the cream-colored sheath dress and examined the elaborate braids that swept her hair away from her face. A simple pendant, from Kraale of all people, rested against her chest, the light-blue, triangular crystal shining even in the dull light.

"Are you ready?"

"I am."

Apparently, people were supposed to be nervous at these events, and while she had to remember quite a bit, she wasn't nervous at all. She'd fought beside Ath'eri, Kraale, and Nysa; she loved Uri with everything in her. If anything, she experienced a mild disappointment at her brother's absence, but that would be remedied soon enough.

An unfamiliar figure leaned against the doorway. "Mind if I have a quick chat with the bride?"

"Not at all. I'll be outside." With a gentle squeeze to Shadi's hand, Ath'eri left.

The woman stepped forward. Dressed in a simple shirt and trousers, she commanded the air around her like Ezra had. Like Judah. She smiled and held out her hand. "I wanted to officially meet the woman gallivanting around with my ID."

"Leida." What the *hell*? "I...it wasn't my choice."

"Looks like it helped. That's all that matters to me." She paused. "You've got a good man. Take care of him."

Returning Leida's smile, she said, "I will."

"Good. Kraale's waiting to walk you out. He seems pretty fond of you. Eibronians don't typically like people outside their own race."

"We've been through a lot."

"Yeah. You're gonna go through a hell of a lot more if you plan on taking down the Embassy. You'll need my help."

"Are you offering?" She certainly wouldn't turn down any assistance.

"I am. I know what my dad did. I've spent a lot of time trying to make up for it. Plus, I'm the self-declared president of the 'I hate Anita Stormbringer Club,' so I have a pretty big stake in all this. Maybe not the most selfless reason for fighting galactic injustice, but what can you do?"

"We will take all the help we can get."

"Good. Now, let's get you married."

***

Floating illumi-globes cast an ethereal glow around the small courtyard outside the hospital. The staff had been beyond accommodating, going far enough to find Shadi a dress and allowing them to use the space for their thrown-together ceremony. They'd even offered their non-denominational clergyperson, but Ath'eri insisted on officiating.

He would gladly take the reprieve. After they recovered, they'd have to head back into nyx space to find Shilah and then deal with the Embassy. The corruption went further than he'd ever thought. He had loved Anita like a mother, but she had to be stopped. He didn't even know what her end game was. With her, anything was possible.

The doors sliding open pulled him back to the present. Leida stepped through, a smile on her face, and joined Nysa. Next to him, Vani stiffened. "You sure about this, buddy?"

"Positive. I love her." He'd already been thinking of her as his wife. Why not make it official?

"Not Shadi. I mean *her*. You sure you can trust her?"

He glanced at Leida, who chatted excitedly with Nysa and Ath'eri. "She saved Shadi's life. Helped us escape. I will trust her until she gives me reason not to."

The doors opening again quieted all conversation. With her slender arm hooked around Kraale's, Shadi stepped into the courtyard and stole Uri's breath. In her borrowed dress, she reminded him of an angel. The illumi-globes highlighted her creamy skin like candlelight and made her green eyes sparkle. She'd insisted on a traditional human ceremony, seemingly for his benefit. After seeing her, he was glad of it.

Kraale kissed her cheek and took his place next to Vani. Shadi handed her bouquet to Nysa.

Beaming, Ath'eri looked from him to his bride and lifted her arms. In a language his translator didn't pick up, she began a melodic chant to which the area around them seemed attuned. Exquisite blossoms reminding him of magnolias sprouted from the trees, and a shimmery powder floated to the ground, creating a circle encompassing the entire group. "Wow," Shadi whispered.

Wow, indeed.

"There. The ground around us has been consecrated to bless the joining of Komandan Uriah Jacobs to his beloved Shadi." Ath'eri gestured to each of them, and then continued. "I will not ask who gives this woman to this man because it is clear you've given yourselves to each other freely. Instead, I will ask, in the presence of our friends, that you join hands." From behind her, she revealed a cord and wrapped it around their wrists. "In Earth tradition, the circle is the symbol of harmony, unity, infinity. It is without beginning and without end. Much like love, which has no true beginning or end." She tied the cord in a knot and placed her hands over it. "The vodni'du also believe that we are incomplete until we find the one who completes our circle, and as I look at you, I see you've reached completion."

Shadi caught his eye and smiled. He squeezed her hand in response.

"In joining hands today, you are joining your lives. No longer shall you be two entities, but one. Your joy shall be his joy. Her pain will be your pain. You will share all things. May you share more happiness than heartache." Placing her hands on their shoulders, Ath'eri said, "Please, speak what is in your hearts."

"Gladly," Shadi said. With nothing but love in her eyes, she said, "You are infuriating. You're stubborn. You're reckless. And, in the beginning, I hated you." The others laughed, and so did he. It was so true. "You're also brave, kind, strong, and so caring it hurts sometimes. Those are the things that made me fall in love with you."

"Oh, are you sure about that now?" he teased.

Defiance sparked her gorgeous eyes. "Yes, you jerk." She took a shaky breath. "I'm not sure where I'd be if you hadn't crashed on Goliv, but I've never been so grateful for a malfunctioning ship. You've taught me how to be human better than anyone ever could have."

Warmth filled him. "I love you, too," he mouthed. For a moment, he didn't know what to say first. "Honestly, if I hadn't crash-landed, I don't know where I'd be, either. Taking you wasn't my original plan. Neither was keeping you. As an Embassy Komandan, I've searched long and hard for treasure, trying to return to the species what their cultures value most. In finding you, I found my own treasure, and I will value you forever. And your attempt to hold in your laughter is admirable."

At that, his bride burst out laughing. "I'm sorry. I...just...."

"I know. Too serious."

"Way too serious. But I love that."

"And now," Ath'eri said, "the rings."

Finally. Her finger had felt so strange for the few hours her ring had been in Kraale's possession, like she was missing a joint or a knuckle. He handed her ring to Uri while she took Uri's from Nysa. Ath'eri covered their hands with hers. "These rings are symbolic of your journey together and are the outward sign of the commitment you are making tonight. May the gods and goddesses of old and new bless your union."

Next came the vows, if Shadi remembered correctly. She'd spent the last little bit contemplating what she wanted to say, what she wanted to promise Uri. He'd made her so many already. "Shadi, what do you vow to your intended?"

What *did* she vow? What promises would she make him? Amazing how she'd intended to stay with him until they found Shilah, and now she couldn't imagine her life without him. "Uri, I vow—no, I *promise*—that I will always save you from fahir and repair our spaceships. I'll be sure to keep cold compresses on hand because we all know how you like to get yourself into stupid situations. I promise to sail the stars with you until they no longer shine, to laugh with you and occasionally let you have your way with things. And, most of all, I promise to love you with everything I have, no matter what."

Apparently, she did well. He brushed his thumb over her knuckles, sending shivers of warm pleasure through her. She couldn't wait to be alone with him.

"Uri, what do you vow to Shadi?"

His smile melted her, like it always did. The heat and affection in his gaze turned his eyes to liquid gold. Lips curved into a smile, he said, "I promise to honor our agreement, to help you find your brother and build a new life. I promise to keep your ammunition stockpiles full, to let you handle all future explosions, and never to let you go hungry or thirsty. I promise to stay by your side through high-velocity ship pursuits and asteroid belts, to protect you when you allow me. You will have all my love."

"Promise?" she asked.

"Promise."

About the Author

Catherine Peace has been telling stories for as long as she could remember. She often blames two things for her forays into speculative fiction - Syfy (when it was still SciFi) channel Sundays with her dad and The Island of Dr. Moreau by HG Wells.

She graduated Northern Kentucky University in 2008 and is still chasing the dream of being super rich and famous, mostly so she can sit around in her PJs all day and write stories.

When not being a slave to the people in her her head, she's a slave to two adorable dogs and blogging at:

authorcpeace.com
facebook.com/lexcade
twitter.com/lexcade